# AWAITING TRESPASS

## (A Pasión)

Linda Ty-Casper

**readers international**

Copyright © Linda Ty-Casper and Readers International, Inc., 1985

First published by Readers International, Inc., New York and London, whose editorial branch is at 8 Strathray Gardens, London NW3 4NY, England. US/Canadian inquiries to Subscriber Service Department, P.O. Box 959, Columbia, Louisiana 71418, USA.

Cover etching by the Filipino artist Ben Cabrera

Design by Jan Brychta
Typesetting by Red Lion Setters, London N5
Printed and bound in Great Britain by Richard Clay
(The Chaucer Press), Bungay, Suffolk

ISBN 0-930523-11-3   hardcover
ISBN 0-930523-12-1   softcover

For Kristina

Books by Linda Ty-Casper

Collections of short stories:

*The Transparent Sun* (Florentino, Manila, 1963)
*The Secret Runner* (Florentino, Manila, 1974)

Novels:

*The Peninsulars* (Bookmark, Manila, 1964)
*The Three-Cornered Sun* (New Day, Quezon City, 1979)
*Dread Empire* (Heinemann Asia, Hong Kong, 1980)
*Hazards of Distance* (New Day, Quezon City, 1982)
*Fortress in the Plaza* (New Day, Quezon City, 1985)

*Awaiting Trespass* is a pasión—traditionally, a lengthy, chanted chronicle of agonies—set in the Philippines, 1981. The agonies in the novel are those of a nation and of a family, the result of usurpations that have turned Filipinos into exiles in their own country.

*Awaiting Trespass* is a small book of hours about those waiting for their lives to begin again.

It is a book of numbers about those who stand up to be counted by trying to be reasonable and noble during irrational and ignoble times; to be honest and compassionate when virtues only complicate survival; to keep the faith when it is no longer clear to whom God is faithful.

It is a book of revelations about what tyranny forces people to become; and what, by resisting, they can insist on being.

—L.T.-C.

# BOOK ONE: Tuesday

# 1

On Azcarraga, which is now Recto but was Iris at the turn of the century when the gray house was built, wreaths start arriving before the body of Don Severino Gil. They are lined up along the sidewalk on wooden stands, until those who sent them—identified by bright ribbons across each offering— come to pay their last respects. Their flowers are then carried up the dark wide stairs and placed before the temporary altar where the casket is to lie.

In order to accord the same courtesy to everyone, the wreaths are moved down the long hall after the visitors leave. On the stone porch, the *azotea* at the back—from which the spires of San Sebastian can be seen through the shiny leaves of the *caimito*, the tree of Paradise—stand the already dying wreaths of the very first to come.

The three surviving sisters of Don Severino arrive in time for a second breakfast. They learned of their brother's death only late the night before, but already they are dressed in full mourning: the same black clothes that for years they have been wearing to wakes—heavy *sayas* with large hidden pockets; *baros* as stiff as armor down the front; and over these, triangular *panuelos* held in place by jeweled pins. Appropriate to those born in the last century, the fashion is as rigid as the garments of saints inside old churches. The skirts are sad and heavy, but just right for January in Manila when the city is cool and *mantons*, for the elderly, are necessary.

The sisters greet, not each other, but the visitors who have lingered in the chance that their coming would not have to be repeated, or wasted on the servants of the house. After a round of kissing and rubbing of cheeks, in quick succession three orders are given to set the table in the long hall that divides the house like a highway.

Then, critically, the sisters and the visitors look at one another, trying to assess how the past is to be resumed for the duration of the wake. All of them appear to be the class of people who are safe from mourning.

With earrings as heavy as pendants pulling their ears, a strange impulse comes upon the sisters to sing. Their voices rise. But like a fixed solitude, a dark star, the death of their brother is remembered. Their hands reach for handkerchiefs deep in secret pockets. Their voices fall and they look properly bereaved again.

"Perhaps he called to us." After some silence the oldest sister speaks, only loud enough to make others wonder what she could have heard. Maria Esperanza is certain it is her name. She and Severino had secrets together. It was even her best friend whom her brother finally married. And it was she more than the others who understood that infidelities become a man; she never chided Severino. Feeling young somehow, her thick hair barely streaked with white, fully stretched and excuding sweet odors to tempt the sun, Maria Esperanza lifts her neck clear of the *panuelo* into which is woven a design of dark lilies. Yet as soon as someone else speaks, she feels old again.

"At eleven last night, I happened to look at the time. Perhaps that's when he died." Maria Paz, second eldest, is impressed with this possibility. She starts to cry, then looks about for the clock that she hears ticking. All the others in that house have stopped telling time and are as useless as the chandelier wrapped in gauze, a nest of sorts above them. "I don't understand it. I never look at clocks. But last night, as if Severino himself made me look. Who else could it have been?"

Assurance does not come from the others who want it for

themselves, though they are not certain any more that such communications occur across the distance of time and other possible divides.

"I look at the clock every time I pass one, Paz. At every one I pass," Maria Esperanza exaggerates. After the other two are silenced by this fact, she proceeds to elaborate upon the lie. "The governor general, a tall man with whiskers like a cat, used to throw his hat at that clock the minute he cleared the last step."

She faces the one beside the stairs, a large standing clock inlaid with mother of pearl and various contrivances to indicate the phases of the moon and the tides. She is not certain it was the governor general; it only pleases her to identify him so. She would have just as easily said admiral, except that Montojo lost the battle of Manila Bay to Dewey in 1898. She does not recall the battle, of course. It was part only of the memory of her father who had stood on the seawall while the Americans and Spaniards exchanged shot and shell. So confident was he in his telling that sometimes people got the impression that it was Dewey who steamed out of the harbor that morning in May, scared and scarred by the cannons on the walls of Manila, by those at the arsenal in Cavite and, most grievously, by the long guns on the battleship *Castilla*, which stood on its concrete bottom in the Bay of Canacao.

Fact and memory have become one for Maria Esperanza, and wish as well, and dreams. "I look at every clock I see; how can you say Severino called to you just because you happened to look at the time? Besides, we do not know when he died."

Or where he died, or why, Maria Caridad thinks, waiting for her two sisters to declare everything so it can be known, and thereafter fixed in the mind. Habits of deference have been born into her, are as old as her bones. Being the youngest, she is satisfied with what her sisters remember, what they know.

Maria Esperanza feels cross because Maria Paz is giving

5

herself such importance, taking precedence for herself. She is, however, distracted from this transgression by the servants, who have set the table and are pulling out chairs for them. Obediently, she sits down, her dark clothes spilling about the chair. Her feet barely touch the floor. Under her heavy *saya* they are as soft and plump as her hands.

They begin looking about to see who is sitting next to whom. Across the table, their voices weave over cups of thick chocolate, which they stir with lightly held spoons, allowing the drink to cool a bit before tasting to see what spices have been churned into it. Memories come upon them in waves, join their thoughts so that they complete one anothers' remarks and anticipate laughter soon enough to withhold it.

By the time the hard ball of Dutch cheese is sliced paper thin – its odor promptly mixing with the scent of flowers and the smell of mothballs rising from their mourning clothes— death is forgotten. Everyone begins to recall things about each other, instead of about Don Severino Gil.

Past occasions freshen sharply like a storm forming in the sea without warning: new slights answer old ones, a turning away when a reply is expected, the passing of dishes out of turn. With some relief the sisters watch their grandchildren feasting at their own table on small biscuits, shrimp chips, pastries and cola. The girls have tiny black ribbons pinned to their dresses. The boys have narrow black armbands at which they pull and twist.

"Bring them over," Maria Esperanza orders, expecting her own grandchildren to be without comparison.

The children crowd the big table. There is much kissing and pinching of cheeks, as each child is presented and recognized. Their poses and light conceits remind the visitors of the parents. Faint resemblances spark excited comments. "I can tell that is Paul's daughter by the way she pouts," one of the visitors pulls a little girl to her; while another one declares, "Virgilio used to hold his head just like this one; and that one has his father's ears. You can't mistake it."

Some of the children are great-grandchildren, removed by three generations from immediate concerns; and the sisters cannot always tell if the correct identifications are being made, so they smile and assume it is their own who are being most admired. Names have ceased to mean anything to them.

Finally the pleasure of recalling themselves in the children fades. Servants carry the young ones back to their table as if they were dolls unable to walk on their own legs.

Anxious to start dividing the responsibilities for the wake, the sisters hurry the visitors' departure slyly by telling them, "Come every day. The full nine days of prayers will be observed after the funeral. Bring everyone." Then in the order of precedence they have followed all their lives, they accompany the visitors to the stairs.

"I'll take charge of feeding the guests," Maria Esperanza says before the visitors reach the lower door to the street. She intends to be overheard in her generosity. Large diamond solitaires bind her fingers as she stands imposed upon her sisters, as large as a major saint on a main altar.

"We can alternate," Maria Caridad suggests sharing the burden. Her rings are *sinámpalocs* or *rositas*, small stones masquerading as a solitaire.

"Nonsense!" Maria Esperanza steadies herself on the bannister. "It is I who have the cooks. I serve better *pancit molo* than they do in Iloilo. And my stuffed *morcón* should be served to the Holy Father when he comes in February." She proceeds to describe the meals that come from the harvest of her farms with the pride of one who has been assigned to attend to the Pope and his entourage.

"What can I do?" Maria Caridad asks. In order not to be saddled beyond her means, she has always avoided taking the entire responsibility for anything.

In any family, there is someone close to poverty in the genteel sense. Widowed early, with no inclination to commerce, Maria Caridad has to be included in her sisters' ventures in order to help augment the income from her short row of apartments. Over the years, however, she has learned to accept the disparities by considering some compensations. Of the sisters, she has the most children and grandchildren in the States. They send her checks inside birthday cards, and on holy days, boxes of delicacies which, on account of prohibitive prices, grow stale in the local groceries. These she shares with her sisters, out of simple generosity and also out of pride: that she is in her children's thoughts.

"I'll take care of the Masses," Maria Paz says.

"Let me share expenses," Maria Caridad is quick to offer, having computed that the casket alone will be several times the cost of any number of first class Masses.

"Since she's the one who's always in church, let Caridad take care of the Masses and you, Paz, pay for the casket and whatever else remains," Maria Esperanza decides. "But, Caridad, not just some churches. All the churches in Manila. The Cathedral and pro-Cathedral especially. The Archbishop's chapel. And don't forget the churches in the provinces of both Mamá and Papá. Include his wife's. And where young Severino was assigned. Every hour on the hour until he is buried, have a Mass said for the repose of our brother's soul, Caridad." She escalates her demands to discover the limits of Caridad's devotion. "Sung masses with *rupekes*, the full complement of sacristans..."

Caridad looks down the long stairs at the end of which, on the sidewalk, sunlight plays like waves on the shore. The metal of passing cars throws the sun's reflection up the treads, against the lower walls. The light startles her into remembering. "It is the thirteenth of January. Tuesday. Sorrowful mysteries. Is it not Mamá's birthday?"

How could they have forgotten? The three fall silent, thinking separately of the festivities they used to have on that day. Long after their mother died, they spent days preparing her favorite food, until they stopped altogether because the children could not always come and the food spoiled, waiting.

"Now, every time it's Mamá's birthday, we will remember

8

Severino's wake," Maria Paz declares.

"Everyone is dead," Maria Caridad complains because she is upset that there is no one else to consult.

The sisters stand quietly, thinking of the two brothers who had preceded Severino, and their youngest sister Maria Fe who died, leaving a daughter who refused to be taken in by any of them, who insisted on living by herself as if she had no relatives, who stubbornly called herself Telly, instead of Stella, their mother's name.

"If Severino had remarried, his wife would be worrying instead of us," Maria Esperanza says, though she rejected the possiblity from the start. "Everything is out of place in his house. Look. Look."

Though Severino Gil had several live-in arrangements, each lasting years, in succession and occasionally simultaneously, these were informal affairs that supplied family gossip without requiring acknowledgment, so he could claim—like their father Doctor Severino Gil who was among those exiled by the Spaniards to Fernando Po in Africa for signing a petition to Alfonso XII, and by the Americans to Guam for refusing to take the oath—that he had given his name and honor to only one woman.

"How much there is in land and furnishings heaven only knows," Maria Esperanza sighs. "We'll have to pay for everything ourselves until Attorney Sandoval finds out, and he will fill his pockets first."

Maria Paz recalls the thousand peso bills secreted in Severino's belt. "Didn't he like to say he might have to pay for his life? I can't think of many emergencies requiring that much."

"It will not help us now. It's already in somebody's pocket," Maria Esperanza pushes a hand into her own pocket, keeps it there.

"Whose?" The other two wait to see what she will bring out in her hand. Their curiosity is divided by the gesture.

'Whoever held him when he died. Whoever was with him.

He could have died in the street, you know." Maria Esperanza does not believe so. Someone with whom he was living – he never lived with those women in this house – called just the past Christmas to invite her. It could not have been with Severino's consent. Such indelicacy! But times were unreasonable. People disappeared, died mysteriously and unannounced. "Didn't it happen to Amang's grandson? They waited for him at supper until the food got cold, and where was the boy found several days afterwards?"

The other two could not follow the sequence of cause and reason but they knew the answer: unclaimed in a small funeral parlor on the way to Tagaytay. By coincidence, neighbors had stopped to rest.... The boy had been a student activist. Such a waste.

"No time for regrets," Maria Esperanza mobilizes her sisters. "We must look around to see what will not have to be brought over from our houses. The curtains! All thin and faded. The drapes will not do for the wake. Does anyone know what happened to the good chairs or where the silver is hidden?"

They despaired of finding anything. When they were still carried about in arms, during the Revolution against Spain and the War with the Americans, their mother had their silver buried before they took to the hills. On their return, everything was gone. Which servant took them, going back secretly to unearth the pieces, was never discovered.

"Some things are never explained," Maria Esperanza speaks for the sisters. "The moment one stops grieving, someone dies." She is thinking of the only pieces saved, those they had brought along, which she still has, heavy spoons made of pure silver that bend in the hand.

"I can't recall when I was last in this house. After his wife died, Severino stopped giving receptions." Maria Paz walks along the windows facing the street, her heavy skirt pulling at the drapes. The large pattern of meadows are like sunlight being shred into shadows as the drapes fall back into place.

"How can people hold receptions in hotels these days?"

Maria Esperanza has discovered a silver platter in one of the drawers. She is holding it to the light. It is one continuous tarnish. "How can fine educated people use spoons some stranger has placed in his mouth?" She directs her sisters to the other tables, to other drawers for the missing parts of the set, while she answers herself, "No one remembers any more what is right and what is wrong. People talk only of what is liberal or not. Pro and con. God is not pro or con. God is what is right. The Pope will be much disappointed in us. There cannot be many good Roman Catholics in the whole country, he will think, since it is in such sad state."

"Have you donated to the basilica for the Infant Jesus?" Maria Paz asks, curious as to the amount. "The First Lady's project?"

Maria Esperanza evades the question. Her son, the Dominican, had warned her, "Mamá. How can you think of giving her any amount? She will build the Santo Nino large enough to be a giant. A Goliath! Save the money for better things, Mamá. Go to Rome one more time. Think of the refugees from Vietnam." Jaime's ideas shock her. A skeptic priest! But is Severino's son, also a priest, any better?

"I will have drapes made," Maria Paz says. "What material do you suggest?"

"Damask," right away Maria Esperanza answers. "Use my seamstress. She can have them ready in one day. Buy red and yellow damask, so in case the Pope passes by he will see his colors at the windows of Severino's house and will bless it."

She looks down into the street where the old houses have become boarding rooms. She can remember when they visited with families up and down the street, not one of those houses being the type that used cotton drapes. Cotton was only for apartments; for houses of third class material, hollow blocks. She disapproves of the way the groundfloors of the residences have been converted into bookstores, all manner of shops, including restaurants. The holes gouged out by

11

rains make her think of graves and she is about to step back into the room when she sees a long black car coming. She is as stunned as if the sun had arrived in a coffin.

Maria Paz and Maria Caridad see the hearse, too. They look at one another and away, rearrange the ends of their *panuelos* around the large pins holding them over their chests. At the sound of commotion downstairs, they begin to make way for one another, end up standing at the top of the stairs bunched together like children hiding in the open.

The hearse stops at the lower door. It blocks the rising reflections of the sun so that for a moment, all is darkness at the foot of the stairs.

Old again and frightened, their shoulders pulled close to their bodies, the three move back suddenly when the stands of electric bulbs are carried upstairs. As in a church procession, they hold their breaths until the entire assemblage passes. This time it is the casket instead of the statue of the patron saint that is brought up last. It is carried with much struggling by thin men, three to a side so that it appears to be rising through a solemn surface, breaking into the light. The polished wood catches the light from the chandelier, forces it to rest upon the surface like recurved horns.

"Where is it to be placed?" the sisters ask one another the question asked of them by the men whose hands, they notice, are too coarse to carry someone who always wore a bouton-niere and light Panama, and wingtipped shoes immaculately white.

"Where?" The men wait for the answer, something close to panic in their eyes, for the wood, impervious to water, has the weight of the tree from which it was cut.

Maria Esperanza points toward the altar, her voice having swallowed the words she meant to say in order to put the men in their place. In her skirt of many folds, she looks as if she is hiding small children close to her body.

Maria Paz faces an opposite corner. Her voice trembles, as hesitant as the sunlight rising to the dark portraits on the walls. "We had Saturnino there, and Elias, too."

Maria Esperanza recovers her voice. Her body becomes firm again, able to halt arguments. "Here exactly was where we had them placed." She stamps a foot. "As well as Mamá and Papá. Everyone." Then she looks up at the chandelier still wrapped in gauze, stands even more decisively underneath, fixing the place.

"I thought..." Maria Caridad starts to say, then decides to remain quiet, speaking the names of their other dead softly, as though in response to prayers being said in the hall. The crucifix on her breast has lost a hand but she does not know it. The gold of the corpus has softened into the wood, an old body melting. "I suppose..." she gives up attempting to remind her sisters that their brothers were waked in their own houses.

All past eighty, the difference in the sisters' ages can no longer be guessed from the wrinkles and the sagging flesh. It remains only in the habit of deferring to the next older.

The casket is slowly lowered from the shoulders of the men who then stand much taller. Relieved of the weight, they attend to the other tasks of adjusting the metal stands so the tiers of light will cast no shadow on the casket. Wreaths are brought forward until the altar almost disappears beneath the flowers, whose scents hang in the air like colored bits of sound. Only the black crucifix can be seen, thrust outward like a thorn.

In the midst of these preparations the sisters kneel close together at the *prie-dieu*. Crossing themselves, they pull out rosaries of many-colored crystal beads. They bless themselves again with the crucifix at the end of the beads then, directing their prayers for their brother, raise their eyes to the coffin and notice that it is closed.

"You forgot to open it." Maria Esperanza leans toward the men, hunching the stiff *panuelo* on her back. "Open it."

The men look at one another. It is some time before one of them comes over to whisper from a distance, "It is ordered to

13

be closed, *Senora*. We were ordered...."

"Impossible," Maria Esperanza says firmly. "How can that be?" It annoys her to be called *Senora* instead of *Dona*.

Maria Paz and Maria Caridad stand up with her but they do not know what to do, so they kneel down again, closer together.

"If they will not open it, we'll have it opened," Maria Esperanza assures her sisters that she will have her way. "We'll see."

Resuming their prayers, the sisters watch the men fussing with the flowers before plugging in the stands of light. The bulbs throb like the pale abdomen of fireflies; swollen buds.

The three sisters blink at the lights, which hold together the long hall. Meanwhile, the men walk out quietly, leaving not even footprints on the smooth polish of the floor.

Outside the house, crowds flow on both sidewalks. Students and shoppers pause in front of the stores, licking ice cream cones or cracking watermelon seeds, dropping shells and wrappers to scatter up and down Recto. The sound they make rises into the house where the sisters are hurrying with their prayers, impatient to distribute grief to those who are coming to pay their last respects.

# 2

Telly Mercedes Palma comes to her Tio Severino's wake in a white dress with bold green splashes that make her appear part of the wreath of white gladioli being carried up the stairs behind her. The way her hair is brushed softly back, the long earrings of matchless design and brilliance, the red lips which look like the mouth of veins leading to her heart, all indicate a care for vanity at the expense of what the still-devout call the soul.

Yet she is shaking inside her body on entering this house of fine memories. Clearing the last step brings her right into the midst of gathered relatives who keep their seats as if a photographer has bidden them to pose and wear a smile—a look of happiness—if they are to deserve forever their foolish and harmless wishes. Each among them has more than what is needed, or earned; yet they act threatened by Telly's arrival. Cousins of the first, second and third degree; cousins by mutual agreement and through marriage all look up expectantly; by act of will, wanting to be the first one Telly recognizes. Everything they do, the way they stand expresses a deep admiration of themselves, and being greeted before anyone else is crucial to this esteem.

Telly misses a step and, embarrassed, begins to throw random gestures of recognition, not caring the least who catches them. God, she scolds herself, I should not have come. She is annoyed that she cannot lose relatives any more than she can elect to lose a finger. On waking up, she had decided not to come; yet here she is, paying her respects not to her uncle actually, but to those who come to wake him. How can it matter to him if he has more visitors than anyone in the family's memory, or if so many wreaths have been sent in his honor that the flowershops in Manila have run out of special designs?

Wanting to feel disfigured to match the hurt she feels being herself, there, Telly walks as if she has never before placed a foot on the ground. Telly has the kind of face that is beautiful when she feels beautiful. Then she practically glows, and the slightest parting of her lips is an enchantment. She holds attention and stays in the mind because she looks desperately sad and yet defiant, someone who would be crushed unless a hand was held out to her; yet the instant she is touched she freezes, her face hardens and she turns away.

This time it is impossible to see her charm for she is not focused on anyone in the hall. Abashed, she wishes to be ignored; wishes someone else will come up behind her and push her to the corner.

Instead she is pulled this way and that, is startled to find herself rubbing cheeks with women she barely recognizes. ''Finina? Of course!'' she manages to say, looking at the fine lips of the one hugging her. Refusing to disconcert anyone, Telly always looks at the best features of whomever she is facing.

''You have learned to lie, Stella Mercedes! How can you recognize me? Since Elenita's wedding—were you there?— I've had my nose narrowed and my eye pouches removed! There!''

They laugh together in appreciation of Finina's forthrightness. ''If I tried to keep it a secret everyone would be calling up each other, 'Did you hear about Finina?' Now that I tell everyone I see, and right away, they think, 'She's merely trying to shock. Usual gimmick to get attention.''' Finina brings her face closer to Telly, challenging her to detect traces of the stitches.

Other cousins have their turn with Telly. Recalling different occasions that do not match, again and again in a ritual in search of permanence, the cousins ask, "When did we last see each other? Where? Oh. So long ago. Really?"

In the excitement of acting happy to see one another, someone always forgets and asks Telly how many children she has. There is a pause, a white silence. Without answering, Telly moves away, her smile fixed like a laser beam. Thereafter she cannot shake off the questions spawned by that one. Children, old enough to be curious, ask their mothers and insist on answers.

Who did she marry? A Palma. The old family.

Who left whom? Why? Men are restless, that's all.

And she? She was liberated before it became fashionable. She thought she was special and exception had to be made for her. The Palmas had money, culture and some integrity. What else does she want? Nowadays one is lucky to get one of those per marriage. I don't bother to check out prospective in-laws. Remember how our mothers picked...Now, if they have fled abroad with illegal dollars, then anything goes, *todo pasa na rin*. Didn't Dewey Dee run off with over P600 million? Everyone does it. Everyone is looting the country. And it's their conscience, not mine...

How many women were there? He still tries to see her. Like a suitor, can you believe?

And? I don't know. She probably has her own lovers. Who?

Their words cut deeply into her and she answers them fiercely in her mind while she moves among them, quietly smiling: waiting for someone to come, to choose her among all the others. I bring my children/Their dead mother, Telly writes in her head, bitter about what her cousins remember and invent. It could have lengthened into a poem, but she reaches the altar where her three aunts are kneeling. She sits in one of the chairs they have vacated, waits until they finish crying. She understands that, from time to time, they must drape their arms over their brother's casket and cry, so no group of visitors leaves without witnessing their proper grief.

"You come only now!" Telly is greeted by her aunts as soon as they get up from the *prie-dieu*. "You are his favorite niece. Your mother Fe, his favorite sister." They wait to be contradicted, while trying to tell her she is remiss in her duties. Accepting Telly's embraces and kisses, each sister attempts to hold on longer than the others. Then their hands slip. They are free again of each other.

Telly chooses to say nothing on her behalf, chooses not to comfort them by saying *they* were the favorite sisters. She pulls away to a seat behind their chairs and fixes her attention on the round table in the middle of the hall. It is covered with a cloth heavily fringed with red. Fading has caused the pattern to appear random, disturbed: a pool into which rain is falling.

"Perhaps she did not get word soon enough? Didn't you get word just now?" Maria Caridad turns around to comfort Telly with an excuse. Godmother to Telly at baptism, confirmation and wedding, the affection Maria Caridad feels arises from special affinities.

"Why do you think he's doing this, *hija*?" Maria Paz turns around, too. "Come around, *hija*. I can't hear your answer. Why a closed casket? No one in our family has been waked like this before."

"No one in any family," Maria Esperanza seizes Telly's arm as she walks by toward Maria Paz. "Santiago was badly disfigured in the accident, but they made him up so skillfully, he merely looked asleep. Was it not so? They are better than surgeons, those undertakers." Her mind grapples with Severino's wake, imagining he must even be more battered than Santiago was, for she cannot think of another reason for being deprived of seeing her brother lie in state. What has some woman done to him? Elias was slashed in his sleep. She cries, but out of pity for herself.

How shall she think of Severino from now on, when most of her memories of him have died, too? The clearest she can summon is Severino as a boy, kneeling at the photographer's studio for his first communion picture. She recalls long silk socks and pants that came down to his knees, white shoes, a rosary and a chain of pure gold from which hung their father's gold crucifix. Whatever happened to the picture? she wonders, eyes upon the bust of Rizal on the *escribana* as if that were Severino's likeness.

Sensing her aunt's feelings of loss, Telly wants to say, "But there can be other reasons, such as respect for the self." In Paradise she will want her own garden. Who wants to be remembered by one's dead face? But is it the corpse that is resurrected? Telly decides she will be cremated. The faith now allows it, according to the Jesuit who mentioned Catholic rites of cremation. Her brother Matias can celebrate Mass afterwards. She imagines all her cousin priests concelebrating... Just thinking of it feels sacrilegious. How can the body ascend to join the soul at the final judgment, the second coming? But wasn't Jesus supposed to be here and now, either never left or returned to wander inside each person?

In any case she wants privacy for the same reason she writes poetry only in her mind; not to have a slim volume with which to enthrall others, but to silence the furious screech that suddenly—with much cunning, always catching her by surprise—twists through her until her head begins to feel like an expanding circle.

The family that does not allow her the right to her own reasons, unquestioningly allows her space and time for reveries as a poet. "She's a poet," is the excuse they give for what she does or does not do. A writer of short stories or novels might be interrupted, but never a poet to whom flashes of inspiration come like quicksilver. Because she is a poet they have stopped trying to anticipate her, to understand how she can act willfully and also humbly, in a shell of extravagance living a simple existence; a nun of sorts, practising vows she never made.

Telly pulls away from her aunts to return to her seat. The three of them, sitting close together, remind her of icons, squat figures to whom one turns in desperation.

"You haven't prayed, *hija*," Maria Paz relinquishes her hand. "Pray at least a decade of the rosary. It won't be too much for your knees. You are young. Go on. Before more people start coming and taking room at the altar. Pray for Severino," she admonishes.

"Yes, pray so our brother Severino will not have to linger in purgatory," Maria Esperanza says. "I'm afraid your uncle did not receive the last rites. Nowadays no one remembers to call a priest to administer extreme unction. They will call a doctor, but not a priest any more. I'm glad Jaime is a priest. He'll certainly come to close my eyes..."

Telly walks to her uncle's casket. The chandelier has buried its light in the wood. She fixes her thoughts upon it. Why will he need her prayer?

A man who wore trouble like a cape, whose appeal lay in his inability to disagree, needs nothing from anyone. God is supposed to love everyone anyway, so isn't it superfluous, a hypocrisy, to pray for what is already possessed? Already promised?

Still, "God, love him. Take care of him. He had good moments when he loved." Whom did he love? She thinks of all the women the family talked about. What other love? She knows of a pet monkey who would not be fed by anyone else, so her uncle had to come home every day from wherever he was to feed it from his hand. Finally tiring of his diligence, Don Severino stayed away for days. She recalls that the monkey died, either refused to eat or refused to live and was buried in the back yard under the *caimito* to which it was chained during the day. At night it had the run of the house, but it perched on the window facing the street, waiting for Don Severino to return. She recalls it hanged itself, or was that an accident when it got tangled in its chains?

He loved but his love did not last. Was that a sin? One should never begin to love unless one was prepared to love forever, and no one else, Telly says gently as if her uncle is listening. He loved her. He gave her everything he thought she wanted. Clothes, trips, money, things she did not need but accepted so he would not be disappointed or feel rejected. He tried to make up for the fact that her mother died early and her father was a timid man who could not believe he made a difference in anyone's life, in their lives, and therefore never tried.

And Quiel? Her husband's problem was that he believed only he could make a difference, so he gave himself to many, pressing female flesh the way others reach for a handshake. Quiel did not have the tenderness and the discrimination that went hand in hand with Uncle Severino's old world gallantry. With Quiel it was a diversion but also a game; scoring points by being seen with the most sought-after women on his arm, by trying to keep the most expensive stable of *queridas*. Indiscreet was the hardest indictment he would put on himself, because as far as he was concerned infidelities were no sins.

Quiel could not make her feel special, the one loved against all human reasons and circumstance; and loved the way she needed to love herself, all faults absolved. Perhaps no man loves this way. Perhaps only God loves this way.

She touches on the wood the reflection of a white flower, an *azucena* from a wreath in the shape of a heart.

Her uncle would have devised some way of being faithful even while amusing himself. He had integrity in his pleasures. Her uncle's way is lost forever, part of the past that is not transmitted in the blood. Her uncle's pleasure rested upon the temptation to sin against God, which Quiel could not distinguish from ordinary temptations.

You're only deceiving yourself. All infidelities are one/ Man is sin. She turns from her uncle to the hall, the room full of chairs and relatives; friends old enough to be considered kin. All those over seventy are deep in mourning and speaking softly. How clearly she can hear whispers, but what is shouted is merely part of the walls against which they bounce.

New arrivals come up, trailed by floral arrangements defined by ferns and glossy leaves. One is in the shape of a

21

lyre; the other, white chrysanthemums, is a dove.

Don Aurelio Gil, a first cousin of the sisters, clasps his hands behind him while Maria Esperanza explains what she wants, in answer to his question, "Where is Sevi? Should not the son be here?"

"I want to have Severino's solitaire cleaned so he can be properly waked...but...his casket will have to be opened. And closed immediately again? I don't even know who ordered it closed. Could Severino himself? But he would have to know beforehand...." It is her answer to every question she is asked. She further explains, "My jeweller in Malabon can add *brilliantitos* to make the stone appear even larger."

Telly decides to remain beside her uncle, to kneel. The velvet is rough on her knees. Bear it/A form of loneliness/A cry. She reaches across the casket for flowers that are no longer cool and wet, glad of her uncle's irreverent disregard of people's curiosities, of the peace of mind of his three sisters who require that their dead be in proper shape to be waked and buried, as if that were necessary for salvation. They have spent their lives, in vain, trying to tame brothers and husbands and sons—succeeding here but not there, succeeding partly and in the end, failing in all of them.

As a child, Telly was told, she would kiss her uncle as soon as he came into the house; that he, playfully, would protest that the young fuzz was being rubbed off his face. "How can I prove to my loves that I had not kissed any one before?" Any reason he had to hide, he came to his sister Maria Fe, her mother. She recalls his coming after a night of drinking, or to hide from an affair that had grown tiresome. There is a picture of her riding him piggyback; of her in a gypsy costume beside his car; of them in a ferris wheel, waving. Like two children, they dropped goldfish into glasses of water to stir the ice, hid fans and spectacles. Once, her uncle even studied ventriloquism in order to startle people who were dumbfounded to hear his voice come out of her mouth.

When she left her wedding ring on the hotel bed in New

York, she imagined her uncle standing beside her, an accomplice at heart. That was twenty, twenty-five years ago; the first time she went abroad to study film, anything to occupy the mind while talk about her and Quiel died down. She ended up taking philosophy courses that she did not attend—but she had the books with her when she walked into the rest home in Katonah. She chose the place because of the sound of the name, and when she walked into the river, that was the word she was chanting to accompany herself.

People say she has his eyes. They have the same sad eyes. He laughed to cover his sadness. Occasionally, she does; or smiles, hiding the hurt. It is not enough that her clothes are bright, happy and expensive. She needs other signs of joy.

Beside Telly others kneel—soft arms and sharp elbows, stiff veils and flagrant scent—finishing their prayers in the time it takes to expel a breath.

Perhaps he's not dead, Telly thinks. Perhaps he's off on a trip, the longest ever, that he always wanted to take. There was never any definite place he wanted to reach. Once she brought the globe to him, demanding that he show her with his finger where they were going when she grew up. He merely said, ''All over, *hija*. We'll go all over and when we get tired of a place, we'll move on. And never stop.''

He was the one she called long distance from Katonah, to tell him she had just tried to drown herself. He said, ''*Hija*, but we must do it together. Don't do anything without me, Telly. Wait.'' He would have gone to see her, she is sure; except that he is afraid to fly – *was* afraid. It was not anything admitted, or expressed. It could be only in her mind. In any case, he sent her money, insisted that he pay all the bills, that she come home right away. He never told anyone about her attempted suicide, not his sisters. It remained their secret.

He would have given her anything she wanted. She had only to ask. Knowing this, as she grew up, she devised things he could not do though he agreed it was worth trying; ventures comparable to going to the moon at that time. All she wanted, and wants (she knew it even then) is a friend who would be no one else's. Failing that, she turns to moments of reserve, of silence, of space she names her own; and through slow disengagements from these to a sudden cheerfulness that is itself not a response to anyone or to anything: often a desolate place where unobserved she can dance, follow the day to its silvery end, begin with sunsets if she wants to, not knowing her own thoughts but allowing them to go on as they will, to escape her body even. A lot of things that happen to her she cannot explain, for they come silently, unobserved.

I bring myself/Where are you? Her uncle never knew how crucial he was to her sense of herself, to her having stayed alive. "You did not wait for me," she chides him now. But he will have his own excuse. What will he tell me? That I must live for him? No. Something more clever than that, something no one else would think of. That she must look for him, now; where he's waiting? The only place she knows is her thoughts.

She discovered this quite by accident, that she can go without leaving, simply by entering her thoughts. She can do it in a roomful of people, in the cinema, a reception for thousands. Yet, she must have known this as a child, for she can recall relatives perplexed that she was more interested in books—in words—rather than in toys. "It's because she did not know her mother." They invented explanations, thinking she would outgrow words and silence. When she was older and continued to read incessantly, they despaired of her ever meeting young men, so they devised occasions for picnics and parties; trying even harder when she persisted. About this time she grasped what she had been able to do, discovered that it is possible really to be in a crowd—the one awaited—and be alone with herself: the central solitude while she took part in weddings and baptisms, *bienvenidas* and *despedidas*, old-fashioned *asaltos* . . .

And realizing this, finally she agreed to be married, allowed her aunts to vie with each other in providing her with a dowry.

24

Quiel was chosen for her, after a fashion. His parents, wanting to intermarry with the Gils, went to Don Severino with the proposal, and her uncle cried as if he were the one losing a daughter. Because her uncle, whom she had never seen cry before, approved of the proposal and of Quiel, she submitted. And for a while Quiel aroused her curiosity. When he lost his, she left him. Did Quiel ever want to be faithful, that he now weeps for his failure?

But Quiel's new and continuing offer of love can only be a way of absolving himself, can only mean he does not remember what he did to her while she can remember all the things that suddenly made her old, remembers the way his breath came and passed over her, his shadow's deep incision, the buried cries of birds. Her memories overlap...I wait empty/Filled with mourning.

Wishing to end all thoughts of Quiel, Telly wonders how she recognized Finina. Could it have been the voice, raspy from cigarettes—a friend mailed her Camels straight from New York to be certain of freshness and because blue seals could be faked—or the neck as long and white as a goose? Radish-white they used to describe her behind her back, envious of her fair skin. A *mestizang bangus*: crossbred milkfish. Swathed in red velvet, in shimmering silk, even in old cotton, Finina used to draw admirers away from them the way a lamp drew moths. A foul succulence, she thinks bitterly.

Telly remains at the *prie-dieu* in order to be left alone, not to be reminded of Finina or anyone else. She wishes she had brought a book, or had a rosary to hold between people and herself. Was her mother's constant praying a trick to be left alone? *Martir iyan*, people used to say of her mother, a true martyr. Why not of her as well?

Telly notices her mother's name painted on a purple ribbon attached to a bouquet of tiny orchids. There are other names. She discovers that the names of dead brothers and sisters are written white on purple ribbons; those of the sisters still living, painted purple on white ribbons. Such fastidious care, she thinks, and in the next breath: I'm forty-nine, old enough to be written across purple ribbons. I've never had a child. Is that not like being sealed in a closed casket? I no longer remember ever having been married. It can simply be a dream, family gossip. A partial solitude . . .

"She must be on her second rosary," Finina comes to get Telly up from kneeling.

"She misses Severino," Maria Esperanza says. "He was a father to her. She ran to him for every little thing. Now he's gone and she's orphaned again."

"What about her husband?" Other cousins seize the chance to learn secrets about Telly. "We hear that he still tries to save the marriage, to talk to her. . . ."

"About that, you know more than I. Have you seen them together?" Maria Esperanza pauses, her fingers marking her place on the beads.

Once a year, Telly thinks, he sends me an outrageously expensive gift; and when we meet by accident, people mistake us for courting couples though his hair has turned gray above his ears. Once, she was disappointed to find out that Quiel's new woman that people were talking about was her. Only me, she thought, the tangle of lives frightening and wearisome. He still cries easily, still insists he loves only her. Sometimes he will even demand that she will require something difficult of him so he might prove it. Something impossible? The last time, he said he was sick. "It's a sickness, isn't it? Let me come back. Let's start over again so I can be cured." But she has her own self to heal, thoughts darker than icons nailed to walls and there allowed to catch dust and grow old.

Her uncle Severino used to say that, like all men, Quiel was sealed with the earth and so he sins; while women were made of heaven so they have the strength to be faithful. "It's the wife's duty to forgive each time a man slips, to help him overcome the earth, the world, so he will not fall so far down. Otherwise a wife fails, is the unfaithful one. If my wife lived, I would be a far better man." She had replied, "You are being philosophical. Nothing excuses infidelity. Not even you, Uncle. And I will not wail with the rest. No one can make me.''

But inside her, she wailed. Every woman younger and prettier than she became the woman who enticed Quiel away. They were married only months then. Perhaps, he was unfaithful even before their marriage. Perhaps he was unfaithful to someone else before they were married; is unfaithful to someone else now. A large part of her no longer felt alive, desired, after she found out about that other woman. She could have become unfaithful, too. Is it because she loves only herself, has found no one else to love? Then why was she hurt, why does she feel she is the other woman when Quiel tries to court her now? What kind of perversity makes her refuse?

In her dreams, after she learned she was being deceived – why should she think she would be the exception?—there were rooms. Sometimes she was outside, the walls of an outer room pressing against her back. Sometimes, she was inside and the room was a dark box that could be lifted and put away. Sometimes, they were ordinary rooms, side by side; but without doors. At each window the sun stopped. Often there were voices. Not hers, the voices spoke sounds that sang but could not be understood.

From these dreams she woke up frightened. She would try to sleep again in order to dream those rooms and voices out of her mind—was that what she was trying to do when she slipped into the waters of the Katonah?—would try to dream instead of flowers, to dream of themselves together while their shyness lasted. But her dreams only turned bolder; a sun seeking places to enter.

The dream followed her. During the day it faced her like a thought, her shadow trying to walk ahead of her. Again and again it etched the woman wherever she herself was standing; it arched the sun wider than the sky over her. She was not able to hide. Her doctor in Katonah said it was one dream actually.

27

The same dream repeating. A dream that had acquired a life of its own. Again and again it pulled her back to the day she woke up in the bed where he had not slept.

She tries to reason with herself. Could you not have been unfaithful, yourself? You have always been in love with someone who lived in your early dreams; and since, with someone who cannot be sealed with earth? She looks at the casket as if it contained those dreams, too.

In her mind she sees a nest of them, several selves dead and sealed with wounds that do not bleed. She is angry that her uncle would tell her submission is what makes women beautiful, desirable. ''Be glad Quiel is a real man who is tempted and has to resist. I have no doubt at all that he loves you, as every man loves his wife, returns to her as to the altar of God after a night with the prostitutes. Every woman has been betrayed, every man has betrayed. That's what original sin is all about. You probably tried to bring him down to his knees. It's a mistake, *hija*. Believe me. I loved my wife so I could not defile her.''

I bore him no children, she thinks; that's being unfaithful. None of those he has by the other women have a right to his name. Her doctor in Katonah said that some men cannot make love unless they are being unfaithful; cannot be aroused except by sinfulness. What is the truth, then; the certainty?

She is being lifted to her feet and led to a chair beside her three aunts. Finina and another cousin are making a fuss over her, telling her not to grieve too hard. They do not tell her who is unfaithful: the one who sinned or the one who cannot forget the sin.

Her aunts pat her hands and order her a cup of chocolate with finger-length biscuits. Hunger is all they know how to feed. They feel her face and neck for fever. Tamed by their concern she sits quietly, a child waiting to be commanded. She feels a chill. The heat of their bodies stops at their hands, cannot warm her. She is shaking, as she remembers shaking inside the river at Katonah.

I should have worn black, she chides herself. She thinks of things too late but the brightness of her clothes has always been indirectly proportioned to the austerity of her thoughts. She lets her aunts comfort her with their hands until she begins to feel that life is made up of old flesh; that she is as worn as they, and older. She rests in their hands until she can no longer suppress a yawn or cover her mouth in time. The yawn vibrates like a sound across the wide hall, drawing everyone's attention. She stands up, suddenly burning.

Without much interest she walks to another corner. Off to one side of the hall relatives and guests are huddled over albums of old photographs. There is much gentle laughter over the poses in which the older generations had been caught. *Tapis* encrusted with beads of various widths and color, hair curled with irons, the endless variety of holding fans and looking innocent greatly amuse the young ones who pull the photographs out to read the inscriptions on the back.

Streaks of sunlight twist across the floor, floating as the wind plays upon the trees outside the windows. Finding the old turntable, someone places a record of plaintive *kundimans* on. It rasps, spinning. Those within hearing pause, lift their heads, fall silent listening.

Telly hears herself in the lyrics about unrequited love. Is that worse than infidelity? When one of the grown-up nephews comes over to bring her hand to his forehead, defiantly and impulsively Telly thrusts up her face to be kissed.

When she does this to the young children with lips sticky with candy, her cousins say, ''Telly really should have had children. It could have saved the marriage.'' This time nothing is said except the nephew's name: ''Paeng!''

A round of chiding and teasing soon enough follow and Telly pulls her thoughts away from the hall by walking to a side window. The bending of the light, the slow turning of the wax record seem as much a wail of sorrow as the stand of drying flowers, the light bulbs' dusty brilliance. She feels it is herself being waked and wonders how many hours of her life she has lived foolishly, senselessly circling, repeating and repeating the things she never intended to do.

How many hours did anyone ever manage to live fully, how many hours in which one was loved back? In this manner, she brings herself to cry.

# 3

Late in the afternoon after classes and other imposed activities of the day, more of the young ones come, lively in anticipation of surprises. Singly and in groups—bearing names like Farrah and Rommel—they come for permission and for money to do whatever they happen to desire that evening. Marvelously single-willed and opposed to all suggestions to remain for the wake, they perform only the acts of respect they cannot forego in the presence of their elders.

Watching them act polite and thoughtful, Telly recalls herself when she was their age. They were called Chita and Lorna and Frankie then, which gave way to Gemma and Ricky. She still has pictures of friends and cousins who trekked regularly to Malabon where, through the use of lighting, a photographer managed to make all of their faces look peaked, movie-star material. Later it was long hair blowing in the wind, straight as grass. . . . How fleeting life feels when seen as shifts from long to short skirts, cycles of skintight and flared sleeves, shingled and bouffant hair beehived like crash helmets. Predominant that afternoon is the innocent tigress look: parted lips and slightly unfocused eyes.

We take turns being young, being beautiful, Telly muses. She is surprised that the young ones are lingering about her after the introductions, returning from the others to her. "I saw you at Efren's," a cousin's son tells her. "I knew who you were, but I was afraid you would not recognize me." The nephew flirts with her, trying to stun her as clearly as she has stunned him.

This is ridiculous, Telly thinks, but does not fight the attention though it makes her feel wicked, someone seducing her own child.

"You were marvelously aloof, Tita Telly. Tell me, what kind of man excites you?" A niece is sitting close to Telly, admiring her. "You look so bistroish. I had your off-the-shoulder gown, the one you wore to the French Embassy on Bastille Day, copied from the newspaper clipping. But that lily in your hair. I could not decide if it was Baguio lily or some exotic kind new to us, so I called. At first, no answer. Then each time the servant said you were not home. Every hour on the hour I called. Then I thought, in your place, you'd wear any lily that struck your fancy. Anything white and stark. I ended up with a butterfly orchid, the miniature . . . ."

The breathlessness, affected for the narration, makes Telly feel drained, and she withdraws into herself, immediately thinking of the wrinkles she daubs with moisturizers at night, careful not to stretch the flesh beyond resiliency. Suspecting the niece is playing with her fears of being old she wonders, How many years are left to me? Or do I look young because I never had children? Or am I really young? The idea seduces her.

"At the Cultural Center, I heard you reading Baudelaire and Gide. Someone said that you never read except in the original. Your French was so perfect."

She is about to explain that she learned the language in Paris where she lived long days in the café and *cine*, drowning herself in the sounds; but her eyes start feeling heavy. An incongruous combination, she thinks: French and sagging eye-lids. So she shifts in her seat in order to edge away from the chandelier overhead that is highlighting her blemishes, and forgets to reply.

"Is Telly blushing?" Finina calls from across the hall. "Look, Susan, is Telly blushing or not?"

"It's a hot flush, not a blush," Susan replies, causing

much merriment among the cousins, who enshrine the remark in their memories.

Telly smiles toward them, delighting herself with her own un-uttered reply: You're all jealous because I am as young as your children. Still, she needs to be convinced of a reason for the attraction she has. The young must sense the rebel in her, giving not an inch of herself to anyone.

She is surprised by this thought. She has never seen herself as a rebel, though indeed that is what she is when she opposes, when she tries to be an outcast in order to feel alive. We all mean to change the world, these children and I, she thinks; the only difference is not in the frivolous or serious reasons, but in that I want to put the world together not as I want it to be but as I think it can be; and this is because I have run up against impossibilities: things which must be left as they are; and they have not yet discovered they can be hurt. Their courage comes, much of it, from not having had to earn their lives.

Should they not be spared the pain? She places an arm about a niece who is confessing that someone she knew from grade school threw herself down from a Makati highrise. "I could not look at her on the sidewalk, Tita Telly. I walked around her, when I got out on the street, pretending I did not know her or what it was all about. On the way down, in the elevator, I was sure she had hurled herself down to warn me. I had finally agreed to go with her to this foreigner...you know, you entertain them for money and for kicks...."

Telly presses her face upon her niece's ear. "She is safe now," she says, consoling herself; for she remembers how it feels trying to speed up one's life past one's own sure sense of oneself, the ache of not knowing when one would ever start being alive, if ever. Having her niece confide in her is like finding a friend with whom a dream is common, sweet with dust but shared. Telly feels possessed of a new innocence. Robert Louis Stevenson wrote that a friend is a gift one gives to oneself. All her life she has wanted a friend to whom she

33

can say what she cannot tell herself. Why am I? is a song of loneliness. Am I? the lovelier form, is sometimes inaudible.

For different reasons from the young ones, Telly feels she, too, has to flee the wake. It stands for something abrupt, undeserved, for lives that repeat and repeat what they try to escape and are caught in poses and shifts in fashion, immune to victories of the spirit.

"Let's go," she accepts their invitation to leave.

"Look what she's doing! Instead of making them stay, she's leading the way!" Her cousins join against her. "She is even more restless than the children and will come to no good. Shouldn't she know better? Her hair is pulled from her face. How does she hide the surgery?"

Emboldened by Telly amid their parents' protests, the children precede her down the stairs. She runs with steps as firm as theirs, not caring in the least that she can slip and end up disheveled on the sidewalk. I can hurl myself as far down as anyone can, she boasts in her thoughts, trying to precipitate new dreams, to go beyond their dying. Hers is the absolute freedom that comes when one is no longer afraid of being hurt or destroyed.

Everything has happened to me, she sings secretly among them; what else can surprise me? This thought brings on its own sadness, for she wants to be astonished. She is ready in her heart for something, has been ready all these years for something she does not know how to recognize or claim: a final rapture of flesh if need be; some inescapable agony; anything with which to feel alive, intensely alive, every pore throbbing, nothing held back. Even something against which to hurl herself, against which to break her smallest bone.

A fragile fire is the phrase that comes to her as she sees her reflection in the glass of a parked car. I really am as young as they, Telly thinks, past marvelling. I am still a child. A virgin child? What does this child want before it is too late?

The answer surprises her. Against her own expectations, she answers honestly: a man. Amused yet frightened by this forthrightness which plunges her deeper into herself, she pushes right into the children: What a wicked thought when Uncle Severino is being waked! What would he have said? That it's a surrender to the world by someone meant to be above sin? Surely he would know that it is not possible to be reasonable and proper when one is being led away to a bright and gleaming place: childless, she should be forgiven for being forever young among the children.

# 4

The men of the family come after office hours, whether they draw salaries or returns from investments. On their way to gambling and other diversions, they make no pretense at grief or praying but linger about the casket, their backs to the altar, and give Don Severino his due by recalling the days and occasions of their youth that continue to freshen their hours. The most impressive remark, the one that has to be repeated for the sake of those farflung in the hall, is that Severino had passed by his friend Sandoval's law office at Escolta sometime Monday morning.

''It seemed nothing was bothering him,'' Attorney Sandoval explains his surprise at being summoned the very next day to Severino's wake. ''But that is the way with our friend. He made light of serious things. When we were in grade school, learning English from the American soldiers, he always made a report on the recent war with the Americans. Insurrection, our teachers corrected us, but we always called it war. To make a long story short, Severino's theme was always those who went silently to their execution. 'Refusing to beg' were the words he never failed to use. And Mr. Smith. . . . ''

Attorney Sandoval looks down at the floor and up at the ceiling. The cigarette is burning close to his fingers but no one points this out to him for the burning seems to be crucial to the rest of what he is going to say.

''That's the truth,'' says Aurelio Gil, among the first in the family to graduate from the College of Medicine the Americans established. For close to fifty years he has been summoned to every illness in the family. From the beginning he insisted on opening every window wide, a change from the times before the Americans came. When parents hesitated, he humored them. "Let the sun come in. The germ is the American devil. However, all it needs is the sun, not prayers." He wanted to become a philosopher, a writer, and everyone agreed because Aurelio Gil liked to meditate; but his parents wanted a doctor as intensely as parents used to wish for priests.

"Mr Smith would ask Severino to leave the room," the attorney continues, "and the two of them would stay outside. Severino never told us what happened. He joked. 'We were just shooting the air,' he'd say. Something like that. But he never stopped talking about that war, about the Natividads, Luna...He did not make them up. He did not read about them either, but he heard about them and perhaps he made them seem more heroic...His stories were what I remember most of going to school."

"He got whipped each time," Aurelio Gil interposes. "He never admitted it or even acted in a way to indicate it had happened. But I remember him wincing when anyone brushed against him. I imagined the bruises were as large as hands...."

"Troubles he kept to himself," Sandoval says, "but good times he shared with everyone he met. In any case, if he knew he was dying, he did not look the part. On his way out, he took another look at the Amorsolo I have on the wall and claimed it was a portrait of the first woman he ever loved. That was news to me. I should have offered it to him immediately. After he left, I thought I would surprise him with it the next time I saw him. But it is too late. My *companero* is gone."

"I saw him Sunday afternoon at the Luneta," another cousin claims. "The Mrs. and I were at the fast food place behind the Cultural Center and there was Severino standing on the seawall. Straight-backed. Like a young man casting his thoughts on the waves. I called to him. And he came over directly to give each of the grandchildren a large bill as a present. There was no indication *this* would happen." The cousin looks at the casket. Close to tears, he blows instead into a large white handkerchief until his nose looks raw.

"He always wanted to die young," Attorney Sandoval recalls, coming back from depositing his cigarette ash on the ferns by the window. "Before he needed a cane, was the way he put it. Well, he had his way. He also told me he wanted to see young Sevi—is the boy in his forties now?—a bishop some day. He loved that son of his, fought against his becoming a priest, then gave in. That's the first time Severino gave in on anything."

"That's true," Aurelio Gil says, returning to their schooldays. "He fought Mr. Smith *mano-a-mano*. Specially when Severino persisted in reciting the American Declaration of Independence after it was banned. Those were the good times. In the course of many lives, unfortunately, things become worse. Now it's our government we have to contend against. I am amazed how people, decent and good people, come to conclude the general corruption absolves..."

"But how did he die? In whose house? With whom?" another cousin asks, clearly trying to foresee his own death, to live the terrible end; then, somehow, live beyond it; making of dying an illness from which one recovers. "Was it quick? A slap of the wind? That's what we used to call a stroke. Or was it pneumonia, the breath of the wind— *nahipan ng hangin*?"

"And why will he hide from us? At this important time when we come to say goodbye to him! a sealed casket! Something is not right, besides the suddenness." Questions come full circle around the hall, leading the men to fall silent, to think hard of reasons that will not frighten away what hopes remain.

"These are not reasonable times. Nothing should surprise us," Aurelio Gil says.

"Perhaps he is alive somewhere. He is full of surprises,"

Attorney Sandoval says. "He can lead the devil in circles. All of this could be from a simple wish to confound us. To lead us to something. It is not beyond Severino! Who could anticipate him?"

"Even Severino respected death. He would not trifle with it," Aurelio Gil defends his cousin.

There the matter rests for the moment. The men pass on to confessing the dead one's sins so they can continue to be allowed theirs: measuring and remeasuring themselves against him as they had done in the past. Somehow the feeling emerges that because Severino, who they assumed would last into the next century, is dead, their own turn is not long in coming.

"Seventy-five in September he would have been," his cousin Aurelio muses. "We were born hours apart, like twins. His mother took the name my mother intended to give me."

"When I saw him Sunday by the sea, he looked almost young enough to be his own son," the cousin recalls. "I didn't recognize him at first."

"His face never bloated up with effusions that augment the virility of some men," Aurelio Gil says, certain the others know whom he means. "His manhood still leaped, *lumulukso pa*, like fish out of the water, but not from taking any drugs or supplements."

They fall quiet again. What they resent most is that they cannot see his face in death. How can they feel more fortunate than this man who gave in readily to the temptations they tried to run from, to which for their own separate reasons they could not wholly succumb. The idea takes hold that somehow Severino is playing with them. They stare at the casket, waiting for someone to suggest that it be opened, waiting to be carried away by the impulse to be certain.

After it wanes and no one has dared to make the suggestion, they retreat to talk about the gold crisis and the decline of the dollar against the mark, about the absence of those who would have been there, except that to circumvent whatever reforms had been made, they have fled abroad to join their foreign deposits, having first taken care to mortgage themselves heavily to the banks they owned or to the government through their connections.

Cigar smoke wreathes the flowers at the altar and the Gilbeys disappear faster than the traditional Marca Demonio gin —as sure a sign of changed times as any—while the men skirmish lightly over political news. Praising changes they have not seen, apologists for the government point to the fact that, after eight years, martial law is being lifted in time for the Pope's visit. Oppositionists sneer that this is only to influence international opinion and only because martial law has been successfully transformed into Marcos Law by amendments and Batasan bills that have kept presidential powers as absolute as before.

When they come close to animosities, they retreat to relatively safer topics. But even on the matter of the free trade zones, the nuclear plant and the American bases arguments ensue. Attorney Sandoval claims the zones provide employment. Aurelio Gil immediately counters, "These are no more than sweatshops where, with no right to strike, with even fewer rights than are guaranteed by Philippine labor laws, workers are paid less for the day's work than an hour's wages in other countries in Asia. American bases, military aid and the nuclear plant being built by Westinghouse are part of the government's defense system. And who is the enemy? The people. America chooses dictators against the people; is the enemy of democracy. No, not America, but its leaders. Perhaps they are also the enemy of democracy in America."

"What more do you want?" Attorney Sandoval asks. "Election has already been promised for this June."

"I want my vote to be counted," Aurelio Gil replies. "In '73, I stood for two days waiting to vote on the referendum, should martial law be continued. The lines were swelled by the very old and sick, all afraid they would be arrested and jailed if they did not vote. The large turnout caused the voting to be extended another day, into Saturday. But that Friday, going home, what do I run into but jeepneys with placards proclaiming 'Yes *ang masigasig na sagot ng bayan*' and '*Yes* is the country's resounding cry.' So, the votes were counted before they were cast!''

"Aurelio. Come. I just remembered," Maria Esperanza calls, thinking up an ailment to draw her cousin away from the discussions. "You remember how Mamá....? Well, the other night, I felt numb all over, down one side. Pain like a ball of sun....''

Having gone through family news and gossip, the women have turned their full attention to the Pope's coming. They require simple certainties. Their main concern is that the Pontiff not be disappointed in the only Catholic nation in Asia. Maria Caridad suggests that flowers in the papal colors be planted along the routes of the entourage, from Manila International Airport through Taft Avenue. What excites her most is that the churches will be ringing their bells as soon as the Pope lands on Philippine soil.

"That should put in their place those denominations who fuss about the ringing of churchbells on Sundays. Why, no one tells them not to ring their own bells!'' Maria Esperanza says.

The others are worried that someone might try to kill the Pope, the way the South American in cleric's robes had tried to stab Paul VI in 1970.

"Something spectacular should mark the Pope's entry into Manila.'' Maria Paz proposes arches, something to remind people of the Marian Year celebrating 450 years of the Church in Filipinas. "Don't you recall the Virgins? Hundreds of statues, some of which I never dreamed of ever seeing. The Virgin of the Salambao, caught in a fisherman's net....''

So various and ingenious are the suggestions that their enthusiasms spill over into suppertime when the pockets of

41

energy in the hall meet at the dining table. At first wary of joining the women's programming of the papal visit, the men soon enough see the symbolic meaning of their desire to focus the Pope's attention on the country's redeeming qualities; and are soon devising their own schemes.

"In honor of Severino then, a last homage to a fallen friend," Attorney Sandoval holds up a hand to silence the hall, "shall we not pledge ourselves, here and now, to repair the church of young Sevi? Then, should the Pope happen to pass by his district, the Holy Father's eyes will light up at our regard for God and His church even in the slums!" If he had thought of it, the attorney would have suggested erecting streams of fire about the church.

The idea receives more applause after it occurs to the family and friends that the press, being international, will be intrigued by slums and slip past fences being raised by the government to hide them from the tourists.

"I'm totally for the idea," one after another, the men endorse Attorney Sandoval's proposal.

"I put down a thousand pesos," Attorney Sandoval declares, writing a check out to young Sevi alongside the tureen of soup on the dining table. He changes it to ten thousand when he hears several others exceed his offer. "Ten thousand," he announces, urgently removing the bananas from the footed glass platter in order to place his check upon it.

The glass platter continues on its way around the hall. Like a collection plate it fills quickly with bills and other checks. And this magnificent sign of their generosity to Don Severino's son so swells those gathered with happiness that, while embellishing young Severino's church in their minds, they eat even more heartily and drink more copiously, easily consuming a goodly part of what they had donated.

"Could stained glass be commissioned and installed in a month's time?" They will postpone the Pope's coming so as to repair the facade and even the sanctuary and the reredos. Like conspirators excited by the daring of their plans, they proceed to plan the refurbishing of the residence of the papal nuncio on Taft Avenue as if they had been appointed to oversee these matters.

They whose thoughts of security depend upon a relationship with those in power are pleased that the projects are in line with the government's desire to show off its authoritarian democracy, Philippine style, to good advantage. Aurelio Gil, certain the plan falls directly into the government's scheme to validate itself in international eyes, lets the platter pass. He could not have topped the offerings, but he could have contributed a token amount. Aurelio never charged for his ministrations—thank yous were mostly what he got—and he even hesitates to accept what his patients offer. His reward comes from his extensive orchid collection which he has built up slowly and which he will not sell or propagate for profit but will press upon visitors, should they show the slightest interest.

As their plans for young Sevi's church seize their imagination, the men begin to be impatient. "When will he come to celebrate Mass for his father?" Earlier they had wondered if fathers did not have the right to live into the future in their sons; if sons had the right to deny this by escaping into the priesthood, abandoning their own lives to spite the fathers they cannot forgive.

The men want to know if Don Severino had managed to summon his son to his deathbed; if Sevi had come, had sealed his dying father with holy oil because they know, friends and relatives alike, that Don Severino threatened and cursed, blackmailed and finally—after much reluctance, the servants attested to this—on his knees, begged his only son not to enter the seminary. Failing this, just before young Sevi's ordination, Don Severino even attempted—again, with much reluctance, the aging servants of the house admitted this—to defile his own son by bringing him to a bawdyhouse on Santa Ana.

Whether or not a reconciliation took place, preceded by

proper contrition on the part of the father and forgiveness on the part of the son—such a reversal of the usual roles—seems to depend upon the execution of their plan to honor the dead father and advance his hopes for a red hat for his son; which plan joins them all symbolically with the departed, while keeping them in the good graces of the government they might criticize but not openly oppose.

So even those who had been offended by the younger priest's insistence on reforms—"The man who has more than he needs is a thief."—even they join in making a pledge, hoping it will also lay to rest the armed struggle in the countryside, the Muslim rebellions which trespass onto their sense of security and peace.

"Won't he be surprised!" All that remains to be done is to inform the son. They wait, expecting his gratitude. While waiting, they go over Don Severino's transgressions which grow more fantastic with each telling. The meek wish these for themselves. The bold confirm their own. It makes no difference to them that Don Severino is lying in state, a mere glance away from the drinking and the laughter. He might just as well have been laughing with them.

Small children, asleep on laps, occasionally are awakened by the exuberance around the hall. Until they are rocked back to sleep, they cry and provide the sole air of sadness to the wake. Those who remain awake and fretful, fall in and out of play. They fight, giving their mothers and grandmothers the chance to act again upon the jealousies and rivalries that had begun among themselves long ago, and passed on predictably to the children.

Women resume comparing children and jewels. Anything below a carat is not worth mentioning. To hear them, not a naughty child was born to any of them, but all their children were filled with the fear of God. None had to escape to Los Angeles to evade arrest, to New York for abortions, to South American or Caribbean resorts to untie marriages. Every offspring is an absolute angel who could have won beauty contests if it had occurred to them to compete; who could have been rivals of Rizal and Quezon; every last one transfigured by maternal disappointments.

Electric fans whir from corners and from the ceiling, throwing grotesque shadows about the hall. Hand fans tip the light. The whirring sound mingles with the warnings, "Never use perfume in jewelry boxes where pearls are kept. Or spray on perfume after putting on your pearls or they will become porous. And crumble. Of course, after twenty years, anything that is not a natural pearl simply disintegrates."

While supper is being served to newcomers, dessert is brought out on small tables. Cool drinks are offered. Since it is still considered impolite to refuse, guests accept what they can no longer enjoy.

Their backs to the altar in order to keep track of everyone, the sisters of Don Severino are thinking of the Mass to be celebrated. Each of them has given a priest to the church and they attach much importance to themselves because of this. Maria Esperanza believes that to be really priestly, a religious has to be Dominican; while Maria Paz keeps an accurate tally of the times her son has celebrated Mass at Malacanang for the President, how many priests he has allegedly helped save from arrest or released from prison since Martial Law was declared.

And yet it is not only Don Severino who is ignored at the wake. The dead one on the cross is useful but not necessary in their lives. Their attention to Him is intermittent, part habit, part playing it safe—in case hell still exists—part of social obligations. His Mass, at which He concelebrates, is no longer a sacred time but one during which attention can be paid to the more exciting details of life. They feel themselves light years away from their own death.

Nor does anyone really remember Sevi clearly. It is as if he is still a child who comes forward when summoned and disappears until summoned again. But they await him because of this father, because they expect to see Severino in him, expect

45

him to astonish them as his father had lifted up their lives into peaks.

The last thing they want—even of a man who has fallen in love with God—is someone who would remind them of Him. Inconstant, they expect God to be constant; eluding Him, they demand that He stand waiting upon them.

# 5

When the discos and beer joints become rooms without doors, boxes that can be lifted and put away—as the galleries and theaters, and supper clubs and ballrooms eventually become—Telly Mercedes Palma has to run: someone is trying to stand where she stands; and every man has become, is about to become Quiel.

It can occur instantly. Other times, she lingers close to boredom before it happens. But right now she cannot run, for her nieces and nephews trail her closely. They chase dark roads for her by bearing down with their headlights, clearing space. They stop to let her speed past them, anticipating her as if they are restless in one another's bodies.

Soon enough they lapse into introducing her as merely Telly, comrade/friend; or *Tita*, letting the new term for aunt be mistaken for her name. Soon enough they give up trying to roll marijuana finer and tighter than she can with her long silky fingers, fine enough to hook light. The freckles on her arms they are convinced are self-applied blemishes to hide needle pricks.

With them she becomes even more absolutely goddess and queen, soon to become they: we, shrugging hips even faster than the music but with the refined and polished hesitations of one who learned French in Paris and Geneva; yet not quite all of life, for her still-stretching body is wary and untamed.

Fast dislocations come upon Telly but she does not wish to be disturbed. Nothing can upset me any more, she chants; the worst has happened to me. She has become a fringe person, outside the action. Her doctor in Katonah said there is nothing intrinsically wrong with that. "It's a choice, like other choices. If mankind was totally satisfied and fully sane at all times, man would still be eating roots in some jungle." A degree of insanity is needed to survive. Some have to be outcasts. Some have to breathe a different air; one that roots in light. Understanding that through her poems she distills air even finer, until it becomes too rare for breathing, he asked her to write one down for him to keep.

She misses his talking to her, his pulling her back to life while allowing her the right to flee. Once when he said she will always be hurt but not necessarily angry—or was it angry but no longer hurt?—she asked him point black, "Would Sigmund Freud say that, if he were sitting in that chair, now?"

My thoughts move white/Among begonias/Rise to that brightly streaked hole in the sky/My days beat like a bird inside my heart/Multiply/Only the tips of their flying/Touch me.

She pulls in more lines through her mind, runs them tight across pages where they will never appear. You/Who say berries are buried in hanging gardens/All they yield are stones/Who attest to alternate seasons/All I feel is cold/I have to stand up to you/Counter you/With my own lies/I tell you/ Bones lie buried in hanging gardens/And the sun/Makes nooses of the grass.

She mocks herself with even more lines until she recovers a trick, so simple it bewilders; she hides in the powder room, holding her breath when they come for her. She hears them running in and out of elevators, distraught that they have lost her. Down thirteen floors she looks to where their voices have disappeared, small on the pavement the waves from Manila Bay cannot reach. Along the seawall the palms are dark flat crowns without stars. She is no longer *we*: but *I* again.

God, she thinks, I'm forty-nine. Should everything that happens to me, anything I do, continue to proceed from Quiel's infidelity, as if that is the time of my actual conception and birth?

No large part of her life can still be remaining. If she only knew she wanted. If she only had some particular longing, an insurmountable wish. She has been described in contrary terms: a picaresque woman, a bitch, someone who has not begun to live. All that she is certain of is that she fears passions that are central to human physicality. She can't even say sexuality. She fears to feel, yet fears not being alive. A woman in Peru, centuries past, wrote about her life/herself; recently unearthed, her book was expertly classified as fiction.

Am I?

She is about to live in her thoughts again, thirteen floors above the sea while on the dancefloor behind the glass doors, retired generals are swinging old bodies to young beats: this one ordered the Metrocom to sweep students off the streets around Mendiola in '71; that one coordinated the armed forces at Malacanang, the Presidential guards, against the students protesting government-occupation of the country. Where is the one who held Tirad Pass against American sharpshooters, who refused to surrender in Misamis? In Santa Barbara? In Bataan?

From time to time, for her, it is necessary—as it is necessary to surface from diving—to live in fantasy, to risk losing the self. Her doctor in Katonah said it is a scared way to live, to be always getting ready to reenter the world but halting: unsure of directions.

She decides to go to Jayjay, who listens to her poems and tells her what the words mean against each other. He says they are full of longing but without intimacy. "You withhold, Telly. Be bold. Be open. Be open and bold, and soar."

Most likely she will meet a woman leaving his apartment, Soho-like in its smells. Soho-seeded. Sophisticated, worldly women go to him the way those who are emotionally empty go to gurus in order to tremble. He will reach out to her the way he reaches out to those women, but before their arms can slide, catching, she will withdraw hers, move away. Wordless/

the sun moves the sky/hides the stars/And I/remain.

Is it because Quiel has her trailed to see if she indulges the way he does? It seems such a flawed reason to hold herself immaculate. That words will stab her. Enough has been said about her, by people even she will believe, to brand her forever. Cousins who will cross their hearts and hope to die; casual friends who will whisper . . .

She has suffered all kinds of molestations: how can anyone claim she has had a protected life? A sign outside Katonah, on a farmhouse gate that swings against itself: Trespassers will be violated.

Something about that reminds her of the wake for her Uncle Severino and she turns the car towards Recto, telling herself that all worlds are simply forms of loneliness. In protest against this truth or lie, she steers towards oncoming headlights to force other cars to swerve away from her. She looks up at billboards to keep her eyes off the road, not caring if she ends up smashed.

How will she bleed against the dashboard? Driver-education classes in the States include viewing films of car accidents, acquaintance with the jaws-of-life instrument with which bodies are pried out of wrecks.

She returns to boundaries. A simplified life is not necessarily a holy life. Merely making small demands on life is not sanctity, unless one makes large demands upon oneself.

While she races towards Recto the dream of rooms without doors pursues her. It comes in daylight, too; but is more insistent at night so she has taken to sleeping in the *azotea* at the back. When the moon is out, the leaves of the tamarind tree descend rainlike upon her. Henry, the German shepherd, rests his paws on her slippers, awake for prowlers who might carry her away while she sleeps. She has tried sleeping in her car in the garage where carriages were kept at the turn of the century. Then, she could have entered the nunnery. It was expected of women. Either that or madness, or marriage.

There is a vow she wants to will herself to make, but she

does not know the words of enchantment that will open the world where one and the hours are pleasant to each other. A Book of Hours scrawled in blood, with ripped edges, lines that refuse to connect. . . .

She reaches Don Severino's house still full of dark, unuttered thoughts circling a fugitive sky. Above the roof of slate no light appears, for all the stars are at the open windows, assembled of flower petals: satellites and galaxies spinning more darkness and hurling blasts, millions of light years away. Too tired to care, she walks against the wreaths waiting on the sidewalk, disturbing the careful design of flowers. The ceiling lights shower the lower door where she looks down and sees her red astonished toes, like faces painted on shell. The odors of sauces, cheeses, drinks and cigars are flowing down the steep stairs. She runs up against them, hurrying as if she is the one awaited.

Midway up the stairs she looks off to the side, distracted by heads massed around a square board where cards are being dealt. She recognizes Dening, the single daughter of Dr. Aurelio Gil, whose son cut Telly across the navel with a razorblade when they were five and playing doctor and patient. She recalls this every time she sees Dening although the brother has died, she thinks in Bataan; or perhaps still is alive, only they have not run into each other again. Dening sees her. "Sssss. Come. We have a fortuneteller. Tell her what you want and she'll tell you if you are to have it. Why do you want to go up there to pray?" The fortuneteller continues to deal the cards. Without looking up from the cards, she tells Telly, "I can also tell you where your husband is this very minute if you tell me his birthday and. . . . ."

"Come on. Tell her what you want." Other cousins tempt Telly. "It's not a sin. It's merely fun. You will not have to confess."

"I'm not afraid," Telly says: God dominates our lives enough. She sits among them. "I want a God of flesh with strength I can feel and eyes I can see looking at me. . . . " She frightens herself with what she says and darts up the stairs, to be free of the thought.

In the hall even more aunts and uncles, mostly in their seventies, are seated waiting for the Mass. Newly washed crucifixes adorn the women's necks. Dutifully she kisses their hands, certain most of them do not recognize whose child she is. I've never felt God, she explains her wish. The hanging corpus on the women's breasts are suns too hot for angels to kiss. How do I feel him? She looks among the flowers for something buried in their odors.

"Will you not join the rosary?" someone calls her deeper into the hall. "Will you lead one of the mysteries?"

"Not yet," she answers, throwing a glance at Iniang, one of her cousin nuns who is kneeling at prayer. Virgin flesh/ Borne without wildness/All you experience/Is God/Who does not come. She thinks of leaving. Prayers are poems memorized to prove one went to the right school. She can say the Hail Mary in Ilocano, Ilonggo, Capangpangan, Cebuano, in the dialects of all her nursery *yayas*. She can say it in English in 30 seconds, in any of its three mysteries ... If she slows down to think of the meaning of the words, like thorns they catch her thoughts and she loses her place among the beads.

I should not have come back, she tells herself. She feels humbled. The hall is becoming a large sealed room, a place of betrayal. And she is no better than Dening, who spends a fortune on having her future told, in trying to have the past restored. She has wasted years sunning herself in resorts which sprawl where fishing villages once stood. Well, most of my life is gone; too late. Is it not mine to spend foolishly? I am they; but also I. She feels saved by the tiny part of her that tries to write in agony, who never has the courage to put on paper what comes to her in trances, while she stares at the sky until it starts to send down roots. I have not hurt anyone intentionally; I have not made a decision I would not make again ...

For a different reason she has to leave. She cannot breathe

52

in the hall. I have my own reasons and they are good, she tells herself and walks away slowly, feeling each step underneath, descending deliberately and meets him on the stairs, coming up large in a white cassock, shy and confident at once, meeting her eyes so intently that she has to look away. She knows without being told that this is Sevi, permanent child, this God-tempted middle-aged man who smiles at her but says nothing to accompany that smile.

Dening calls to him. "Father Sevi. Come and have your fortune told." Her black clothes make her seem to be the daughter of the house. Her habit of holding one arm across her chest makes her appear desired, fighting advances.

His smile breaks into a quiet laugh, so full of good will. "It's not for me," he says, looking away as if he cannot bear human contact.

Telly thinks he says something like this as he turns to her on the stairs, stands there as if waiting for her opinion while those in the hall are waiting for him, awaiting him as in prophecy. He takes the time to stand there and wait for her to say something instead of merely standing still like a tree waiting for rain. She turns and follows him up the stairs. It is as if he has called her by name. Speak for me, she thinks. And she is filled with longing that frightens her with its strangeness. I must not think of him as one who can desire, be made to desire. He can't defend himself, he does not play our games.

She is smiling when she stands beside him in front of the three sisters, smiles scolding herself that she wants merely to be desired so she can let go and watch it all come to nothing. Need I warn him, she pursues the thought, this inexperienced child-man who halts at the edge of life? Where he stands/ There is not enough ground/For one beside. Is it true of herself as well?

# 6

As soon as Father Sevi is heard coming up the stairs, the other priests in the family are called from the back room where poker tables are set up. The young children stir in their sleep. Despite the muffling of voices, they feel the commotion and think a meal is being set, but sleepiness wins over.

The older women, who take their devotion seriously, pull out their beads. No longer able to kneel at length, they sit small in their chairs, waiting for Sevi to come to them and receive their blessings in return for his. They admire him with their eyes. "He is devout," they whisper. "He looks like a Christ."

Remembering their plans about his church, the men interrupt the preparations for the Mass. "Sevi. Father," Attorney Sandoval reaches for Father Sevi's arm. "We have something you will like. We have in the course of the evening come to the conclusion that, in honor of our friend your father, and also because the Pope is coming, thinking of your father's wish for you, which being his is also our own since you have been like our own son, we have decided, and upon this I admit we have acted hastily but with good intentions, that we will have your church repaired, put into such shape that when the Pope passes—and certainly he will ask to see the slums—he will be properly impressed with our care for the faith, with our regard for God and everything that pertains to Him. So, I have the honour to present to you...."

"Would it not be more proper to bring it up after the Mass, or during the collection?" Maria Esperanza suggests too late, because she did not think Attorney Sandoval would have done anything without first letting her know.

"But this is not in the church, should there be a collection?" Maria Caridad asks.

"Well, I've already made the introductions, so let me finish," Attorney Sandoval says, calling for the fruit platters to be brought forward so he can present them and so Sevi can be grateful.

Sevi takes the platters, saying nothing. For a long while it seems he will say nothing, might even refuse to accept the money. He is thinking that if they really meant to help his church, they would have thought of helping the people instead of repainting the facade and landscaping the church entrance as Attorney Sandoval continues to describe. But Sevi knows that if he says what he thinks, they will be hurt. They will think he is rejecting their good intentions.

"Say something," Maria Paz urges.

"Should there not be enough to do a good job on the church, I will make up the difference," Maria Esperanza offers. "Say a few words, then, so we can have the Mass. People have been waiting."

*Lagi na lang nagpúpuno*, Maria Caridad thinks of Maria Esperanza, always "making up the difference". *Maliban sa kanya, may kakulangan ang lahat*, each imperfect except for her, Maria Caridad adds resentfully, is immediately ashamed of her thoughts, but she owns them.

Sevi hands the platters to a servant who has cleared the altar of flowers to find a place for the donations. He turns back as if to say something, then changes his mind and goes to the inner room where his cousins are putting on their vestments. He carries his own on his arm.

Telly thinks she knows what Sevi was struggling to say. We are much alike, she thinks, for she remembers that Sevi has been raised in the house next door, in the hut that was finally razed to make way for a *cine*. Because he was rarely home, Severino's neighbors agreed to look after the small boy. She thinks she has heard someone say Sevi is not really Severino's son, how or why she cannot recall, only that relatives are certain only of the children of the women. In any case, they both grew up abandoned, orphans obliged to live without physical love, with no apparent object of love. But life supports a variety of love, she tells herself. That she feels she has been deprived need not be his feelings. How contemptible you are, she scolds herself; all you want is to be desired, but you do not love back. It's very possible you forced Quiel to become unfaithful by demanding his absolute love which you did not return; absolute meticulous love that makes a fetish of faithfulness. You used to eat in silence, she reminds herself. You sat across from Quiel while your thoughts escaped. . . . Free from sin but/Nevertheless/Unfaithful. . . .

Sevi is holding out his hands over the gifts on the altar. "God of power," he says, shaping each word full of meaning, "giver of the gifts we bring, accept our offering, make it the sacrament of our salvation. We ask this through Christ, Our Lord, from whom all good things come. . . ."

Telly lowers her gaze from the chandelier. It is as if she is hearing the other half of her thoughts although she cannot recall a word that is being said in prayer. Are we the same person? she asks herself, looking up at the chandelier because she cannot bear this thought. The servants have forgotten to unswath the lights, so used to the cheesecloth have they become. To look at us, however, we appear to be opposites, but it's the same life, lived inside. Somehow they have escaped the power of the world. She blinds herself with fantasy and dream; failing that, with anger. How does he harden himself against externally exciting things? Are we both merely afraid, strong-willed in fear? Is there a purpose in willfulness beyond merely opposing?

She hides her eyes in the folds of dust, her thoughts in what she has been told about her mother: dressed for internment in her wedding tiara and gown, white butterflies with mother-of-pearl bodies and wings of beads sliced thin and transparent.

She cannot bring herself to mourn, for she envies her mother the courage she does not have. I'm not as brave as she, she imagines herself telling Sevi so he can ask, What courage do you mean? Does he imagine her when she imagines him? In their halting and circling how will their thoughts discover each other? And what then? She tries to recall a prayer, for herself, but fails. Never mind, she consoles herself. God cannot be the answer for everything. To whom can I call then? In what, in whom can I believe so I can know what to expect of my life?

She hears children being asked to bend their knees and she kneels in obedience to the same command. She has no way of knowing if her mother really killed herself. Next time, let's do it together, she whispers to the one whose voice she does not remember.

"We come to you, Father, with praise and thanksgiving, We your people and your ministers...."

Telly feels herself being prayed over. Are we the gifts, too? She thinks of the crutches at Lourdes, the offerings of thorns from poor and broken selves. I am as broken as they are, as imperfect, she thinks. Shall I offer him the bones down my back? The dark walls make her feel she is inside a church, joining in the celebration in order to deserve earth first, then heaven.

Such a strangeness comes over her as the gifts are being consecrated. She feels herself being entered, along with the words, with the presence of those words; a feeling so different, so full of temptation that in her fright she uncovers her knees and stands up, trying to break the power of those words before they lead her to abstain from herself. She stands up wondering what will separate her from the others in his eyes. Unabashed, in the middle of the liturgy of the Eucharist—having thought she had outgrown desire; having dreamed herself ugly night after night—she stands there demanding that he judge her beautiful, wanting to stun him.

You/Who stand there/So full of goodness/In whom the Lord is pleased/If I could know/You see me/I would not need to be/Perfect.

57

# 7

Sevi did not see her stand unabashed, waiting for him to look up from consecrating the bread and wine. In those moments, if he saw anything, it was his thoughts centered about the words of consecration. He did not see his hands as he spread them over the specie, turning them in that most mysterious of mysteries into the Body and Blood of Christ.

So, he cannot entirely understand why his aunts tell him not to mind her. "She does what she pleases. We've tried reason with her," Maria Esperanza says.

"We tried, in place of our dead sister, Maria Fe. Her mother, you know, was a sainted woman who never opposed anything in her life. Estella, perhaps from her father's side of the family and since she was young, always opposed. She might say nothing, but it does not mean she is going to obey. I don't know how many rosaries I said for her . . . ."

"Your father tried, too," Maria Paz adds. "He talked to her for hours. Neither, I suspect, was listening to the other. They both of them have that stubbornness. Although I recall Papá had that himself. Once something got in his head, no one could take it out. You could beg and say your beads all night – nothing could dissuade him. Mamá used to say it would take a miracle . . . ."

"Maybe you can talk to her," Maria Caridad says.

"Yes, try to put some sense into her head," Maria Esperanza adds, taking over her sister's idea. "For our sake, talk to her the way your father did. She might listen to you. She can be married again. Maybe, if you offer to celebrate the Mass. If we can see her married and settled, that will give us peace of mind.''

''Yes, that will give us peace of mind,'' Maria Caridad repeats. ''She is after all, our own sister's daughter. And she has no one really. Matias, her brother, is a priest and he can't talk to her. She is stronger-willed than he.''

''Find a way to talk to her.'' Maria Esperanza pulls at Sevi's arm. ''But now, I think you should say something about the offering Attorney Sandoval presented. Say you're grateful, which I'm sure you are. It does not hurt to be humbler than you should be. Approach him. He's at the table. Sit beside him and say you accept it in the memory of your father who . . . You know. Say what will make him and the others feel appreciated. Then they'll probably give more. Do it now, before people start leaving. It will make them feel good. They waited for you because you're Severino's son. Now, go ahead.''

It is not in his nature to speak what is not on his mind. What he wants to say is not what they expect to hear. He wants the money spent on his parishioners instead of on the structure. It's not a first class church building by any means and making it appear like one is at best hypocritical. But the money, used in scholarships to deserving students or to feed those who taste meat only twice a year or to house those who live in cardboard huts on stilts over the swampy ground, would help some live decently, a human right even more important perhaps than the right to vote. Many in his parish have never felt God's love, only what they consider to be His anger: illness and misfortunes. The mystery of His living flesh is probably reduced to the level of magic for those who cannot tell if they are in God's thoughts, if they are really part of His plan of redemption and salvation, the hope of heaven. What a waste of life poverty and human misery are!

The last thing that will open their hearts to these facts is for him to declare them. He will just have to be patient, Sevi thinks, somehow lead them to discover on their own that God is faithful not to structures, not to institutions, for He did not create these. But He created people and He is faithful to them. The people are His church on earth.

Bert Gil, who has contracts in Saudi Arabia and Singapore and Thailand, comes to Sevi. "Before I leave I want to warn you that stones can be put together any old way, but there is only one right way. For that you have to go to the experts. The sisters have told me that you should have a presentable church and that the contributions you get are all in small coins. Well, first of all you need a simple design, let us say. But a good one. Let me provide it for you. I will coordinate with Simeon, who is the architect. He should come sometime. Together we'll hang the windows and doors right for you. That's what cousins are for. And you're welcome to the house anytime you think of coming over. There is also, always, an extra car in the garage. Use it for whatever. But this is just the beginning. Anything you need, ask. I can get it for you."

Sevi holds his hands locked across his body, like an old priest dozing. His face has lost its gentleness, for he is struggling to keep from saying that excess deceives a man into thinking he is already in heaven. Bert will consider that a harsh judgment.

Attorney Sandoval joins them. "Good. We'll let Bert take charge of construction details. We'll have no fear of bankruptcy. His contracts are all guaranteed by the government, so we're all set. Malacanang is behind him."

"I'll donate concrete," a cousin offers. "Let me know how many bags." Another offers lighting fixtures. Yet another donates tiles and others, carried away by the moment's generosity, insist on giving Sevi what is not needed for his church.

Attorney Sandoval takes matters in hand. "Money," he advises, "is preferable. Where will all those things be stored? And if they prove to be unnecessary? But money is always useful." He also reminds them that Sevi is coming into a substantial amount himself. "Though this should not deter anyone from giving to the church. But I want to take this occasion to remind Sevi that he should not spend what he is to inherit on charity entirely. Live a little, son. A car. A trip. Good friends. That's what your father wanted for you. A taste for the good things in life. I remember him saying that I must take my own children to the best restaurants so they will get used to the best and will work hard to be able to afford them. You can live for your father, a little, I think. This house, for example, will be yours. . . . ''

''You will not sell it?'' Maria Esperanza asks. She has thought of Severino's property but not of Sevi as his heir. ''It has been in the family since it was built. Papá lived in it himself until he died. He and Mamá moved here from Ermita. . . . ''

''It will make an excellent hospice,'' Sevi says.

''A hospice!'' The idea surprises Maria Esperanza and shocks her. The word assaults her tongue. ''A hospice? Of all things a hospice. This home turned into a house for the dying?'' Her sisters cannot bear the thought either. *''Hindi sa matapobre ako*. Not that I look down on the poor. . . . ''

Maria Paz comes to touch Sevi's arm. ''Think of it some more, *hijo*. Is that what your father would have wanted? Who will it help? Not the church certainly.''

Maria Caridad whispers to Sevi, ''Decide later. Wait until the wake is over. Then people will not feel so displeased or angry. Say nothing more now. If that is what you really want, I understand. What can you do with an empty house?'' She is saying this because she was touched by the way Sevi said Mass. She felt very close to God when he raised his hands in blessing. It was as if he had prayed in Latin. She was reminded of the old church where she was baptized, which was carried away stone after stone by the river.

''A hospice is not such a bad idea,'' Aurelio Gil interposes. But no one agrees with him. He is the last person to dissuade the family because they think all his efforts to understand with the pure objectivity of reason have no bearing on

61

the ordinary and persistent events of life. "Is this not so, Telly?" he turns to her.

"I like the sound of the word. I have nothing against a hospice," Telly answers. She has always thought that there is a certain majesty that comes to those who do not hunger for things. They seem most alive to her, those who resist the world, who take risks against themselves. He has very little to recommend him, she thinks of Sevi. He neither sings nor plays a musical instrument. He cannot talk about movies or television programs; or trips or politics or the arts. And yet there is a certain forcefulness about him, a clarity. The look of a prince, she concludes, turning her smile on him. Their hands are the same shape, she notices.

As if greeting for the first time someone not quite known to him, he merely nods but does not go to her. He is wary of confrontations, having had enough with his father and with himself. Afraid of his anger, of breaking apart because of the hurt that has lived inside him, he cannot face the doubt that he is Don Severino's son, because he cannot reconcile being that son and having been raised in the hut next door; being that son and looking up at the windows of that house, at which his father sometimes appeared, and sometimes called for him to come up and receive a coin. If he is the heir, then he must be the son; but if he is the son why did he live in the hut?

His anger comes to him fiercely, a bull to be wrestled to the ground. Only in the intensity of God's love has he found any peace.

The woman who called him on the telephone said his father had left instructions for his casket to be sealed. Was it to repudiate him further, even in death? And his own decision to turn the house into a hospice, is that unconsciously to spite his father, to repudiate him in turn?

And then there is Telly, who looks at him directly as if she is looking at herself; restraint dissolved in familiarity; and he feels he knows her, when he does not. What can the three sisters possibly expect him to say to her who obviously is used to attention yet is trying to catch his? She stands apart, like the women in the Bible waiting to receive back their dead . . . before resurrection.

Now she is looking away; perhaps did not see him at all, did not recall their having met on the stairs. There is no feature of the Gils between them, as far as he can see. Why does he feel the same blood runs through them? If not that, the same fury. An uncanny feeling comes to him that they are the only two people in that house who are thinking of each other, even as they stand apart, looking in separate directions, even as she is walking away.

Thinking it is out of willfulness that he stands his ground, Telly turns away and leaves the hall, though she wants to wait until he comes; wants to, knowing he might not. Leave him alone, she tells herself: You will merely turn him into a toad; uncreate him. Enough, enough, she tells herself, speaking in a voice that is as painful as light trying to force apart the darkness.

Yet it is for his sake I think of him, so he will not be someone who has lived unguarded in the fields, unloved. But what good is it, not knowing one is loved?

"It is impossible," Maria Esperanza is greeting those who are just coming in, with the announcement of what the son wants to make of his father's house. "A terrible thing amounting to disgrace."

"He cannot mean it," the guests console Maria Esperanza. "He will change his mind. *Que horror!*"

"It has always been our house," the three sisters of Don Severino look about the hall where they once danced and laid their heads on many carefree dreams.

"I will not permit it," Maria Esperanza breaks away from the past and her memory of it. "For Severino's sake, I will not permit it." And she leads the newcomers to the casket. Passing Sevi, she thinks of bending him to her will and tries to faint, but her strong heart refuses.

# 8

As Maria Esperanza darkly prophesied, the offerings and Sevi's plan to turn the house into a hospice divide the family. Into the night the discussion goes on. Determined not to be persuaded out of their opinion, people doze off in their chairs, wake up to resume their argument. Habits of obstinacy and domination, old frustrations compel and impel them after their bodies have succumbed to weariness.

So like family wakes before, Don Severino Gil's also becomes a place of hurt feelings and enmities. Recriminations pass back and forth as positions become as solid as the stands of lightbulbs shaped to simulate candles.

Having caused the dissension, Sevi remains in the house to bear the results fully. He is assailed by conflicting views claiming one faith. Their eyes and hearts are set only on their gain. Make me faithful, he prays; justify me. This is the first time he finds himself in the midst of his father's gathered family; the first time he is centered in their attention, the one to be won over, the trophy claimed by all. In the past he had often wished to be claimed this way. Now he feels himself rejected, just another point of dissension.

During one of the many silences, truces imposed by the lateness of the hour and the arrival of new mourners whose loyalties are immediately to be tested, a distant aunt comes over to Sevi. ''I'm on your side,'' she whispers to Sevi. In full view of the others, she takes off her diamond earrings and drops one each into the platters filled with offerings for Sevi's church. ''We must not give from our excess. We must give until it hurts." She does not say that she almost lost the earrings on the way to the wake. One was snatched by a thief to whom she had the presence of mind to call out, "Take the other one as well. They're just glass anyway," and the luck to catch the earring as it was thrown back.

The rest are briefly impressed by her gesture, then resent it and turn to other matters in order to ignore her. During past administrations, she represented the country abroad. Naturally outspoken, she revels in talking about the dangers of power. Though no one listens, she turns the matter of the hospice into the dark attraction that power has over ordinary men. "It overcomes reason and will, this thing that corrupts and makes leaders think of themselves and of their friends whenever the word *country* is mentioned. Except for the power to serve and to heal, all others corrupt and degrade those who wield them; but power attracts. That's the appeal of martial law. The mystery of unreason, of men saying one thing, yet clearly opposing this in everything they do."

"The way to silence her is to have the President designate her Batasan member or appoint her minister," Attorney Sandoval says under his breath while appearing to listen with marked interest. "Then she'll sing an entirely different song."

"If the administrators of martial law were really concerned about the country they would not have allowed the Kawasaki sintering plant," the aunt continues, leaning toward Sevi as in confession. "The Japanese refused to have that steel filtering process in their own country, because it's ecologically unsafe for all kinds of life."

Sevi leans away to be able to see her more clearly across the distance of two armrests.

"But we hold life cheaply here. Pesticides, herbicides, tainted milk—anything unsafe in the world finds its way to the Philippines. That nuclear plant Westinghouse is building cannot pass safety inspection in the United States. Do you realize where the power lines are going? To the American bases, to the export processing zones where foreign industries, which do not pay taxes or come under our laws, can exploit Filipino workers. They take their profits home, too.''

Sevi sits up straight in his chair, feeling guilty that he has not been fully aware of these facts. They should have concerned him as much as his parish.

''And I might as well say, for whatever good it does, that if we do not stop selling our trees to Japan, we will be importing lumber by the year 2000. That's in less than twenty years! What a patrimony we're leaving to future generations! This waste of our resources, and martial law! I see the apologists for the powers-that-be are shaking their heads. Look at that Sandoval. He was Severino's friend. Watch. He'll help himself generously to your father's property. What are friends for, he thinks. Well, you have to learn to take care of yourself. No one else will do it for you. . . . Now I must go.''

Sevi holds the hand she reaches out to him and gets up as she does.

''Young man, be on your guard. I wish I could be convinced that prayers would solve our problems. At the moment, however, that seems to be all we've got. *Ave Marias*. Perhaps the Pope will perform a miracle. What is it, that noisy prophet Jeremiah lamented? Free us from the hand of the wicked, the grasp of the violent. You're surprised I know some scripture. I was a sickly child. Polio. The only book we had was the Bible.''

Sevi wants to say something, impressed as he is with his aunt.

''Now, accompany me. I must say a prayer for Severino. Did anyone say you have your father's ears? That's the Gil ear. All the men in the family have it. Even Aurelio. And the strong women, of course. And don't believe just anything they say about your father.'' Now she raises her voice. ''Severino was a far better man than any one in this house, right now.''

''Bravo, *companera*,'' Attorney Sandoval claps.

"Only entertainers are applauded. I am not one of those kind," the aunt thrusts her chin, speaking even more decisively. "There is no reason to change or amend my opinion. Anyone can govern in martial law. A man of not much wisdom or courage commands because he cannot persuade. He does not have to be right, though being right is not an excuse for absolute power. So!"

She goes to the casket on Sevi's arm, crosses herself. A moment of silence, then she goes to the three sisters and is headed towards the stairs. "God Himself does not force us to love him. We can refuse. I see, you have not refused Him. Be a good priest."

Sevi wishes he had known her when she was younger, that he knew more about her. Too late he thinks of accompanying her down the steps, of leaving with her. All he can do after seeing her to the stairs is return to his seat.

The sealed casket does not worry him as it does his aunts, for that would be like worrying about the body when it is the soul, the spirit, that ascends, which is the real mystery.

He can hear them measuring him against his father, their voices like rings digging into his hand or stiff *panuelos* scratching his face. Those who agree with him about the hospice are saying no one should be surprised or offended, "He's a man of God, let him give his inheritance to God." Those who oppose the idea answer, "The house means nothing to him, that's why he can throw it away. A real son would not think of this. Wait till he realizes what he's doing. He's young yet."

And they come to him by turns, trying to get him to yield.

A servant comes to Sevi. "Your aunts want to know if you will not sleep in one of the rooms. Will you make your choice so the others can be assigned their beds?"

He answers that he will stay in the hall. "Give the bed to others." He is bitter that their attention is to small details. No one has said his father's name except to call attention to themselves. "I and Severino used to do this.... *I* said to

Severino. . . . He always came to *me*. . . ."

"Will you not change your mind, Father?" Another message is sent to him from his aunts who sit across the hall, surrounded by relatives. Food is pressed upon him. He answers that he has had enough. They cannot understand how anyone can be content with enough.

He gets up to stand at the window overlooking the street. He has not intended to stay after the Mass. In his parish there is always someone calling for the priest, someone needing to be given the last rites, some fighting he has to mediate and to stop, families to bring together somehow; someone asking to be confessed after stealing or killing. . . . He has been living in the midst of crime and dirt and illness. They are his family and he misses them in this desert of his father's house where, attempting to be the bearer of the good news of God, he has set his father's relatives against each other, set them practising old tyrannies.

All he wants, humbly, is to have others experience God through him, but he has caused them to sit separately in the hall, like besieged cities.

# 9

The three sisters decide to sleep in their brother's house. The thought alights upon them like a bird. For some time, the making of that decision interrupts their concern about the house being converted into a hospice. The decision is reached when the sisters remember the difficulty of mounting the stairs. "Besides," Maria Esperanza says, "we will no sooner get home than we will have to turn around and come here. But, I have not been able to sleep except in my bed...."

Aurelio Gil prescribes *serbesa negra* for the sisters before they retire for the night. Beer is his usual and gentle prescription for almost any woman's complaint that does not need surgery. And he is one of the best diagnosticians in the city. From him young practitioners learn what they had missed in their training.

The sisters follow their cousin's prescription selectively. None of them likes beer, but they dote on a sip of wine before going to bed. *Mompo* and the rosary have been putting them to sleep.

The rooms are chosen with some ceremony. The linens are brought out and the beds made, only to have the three decide, after all, to sleep together in the same room. It might have been their intention from the beginning, the servants reflect on the waste of their time, but will they disclose this to anyone? The servants think it is part of the pretense of having the rosary said all day. Such prayers are no longer said so rigorously; and wakes in funeral parlours or chapels have become acceptable and popular.

Despite all the elaborate preparations, the three cannot fall asleep. They turn and twist their blankets. As if they are bothered by separate ailments, they take turns sitting up in bed, then going out into the hall only to return and sit up some more, staring at the darkness.

To Maria Esperanza the large room feels like an old garden at night, when nothing moves. She pulls herself up against the headboard. A strange odor has awakened her from sleep. Inhaling, she waits for certainty before waking the other two. The smell makes her think of withered flowers, but she finds no trace of it in the room. Their mother had the habit of sleeping on flowered necklaces of *sampaguita* that she wore during the day, and Maria Esperanza wonders if it is that sweet white scent that broke into her sleep, that has again started to weave inside her body, making the room appear to be an old garden with all the grass pulled root by root so snakes cannot glide so quickly in.

That she cannot identify the odor convinces Maria Esperanza that something is wrong. She connects this smell with the sealed casket. Notwithstanding the explanations that have been made during the day and which took away the edge off her fear, she returns to it now. She is certain something has been done to Severino—by an angry husband? a jealous rival? —and that the what and by whom must be ascertained so that the family can be properly avenged. Suppose it is the government! She runs away from the thought. It is not possible, she tells herself. One of her sons is a general. And besides, Severino never bothered with politics.

She blames Sevi for her fears because, she thinks, the idea of turning the house into a hospice has induced them. In any case the son does not have the father's presence that assured people and made them feel all is well.

Maria Esperanza decides to recite her rosary. The length of beads binds her hands together. While blessing herself with the crucifix, she looks at her sisters, who remain still on their beds. How can they sleep through her fears? She can feel her heart beating in her head. She slides down, pulls up the covers and lies the way she did as a child, waiting for something to come out of the darkness. She can taste the absence of light. It is the taste of dead wells. Her thoughts return to all the wells she has ever seen dug, to the river that divides their town and slams grown trees against the bridge during floods, carrying away the railroad tracks and planting them where trees have been uprooted.

It is strange, she ponders. One does nothing at all in order to be born; one does nothing and one dies.

She turns to tell her sisters this, but if she does, they will only insist that they smell nothing. They will say this so they will not have to be afraid. Everyone in the house is someone through whom her blood flows, yet only she has smelled the odor.

Then Maria Esperanza turns to the matter of the hospice, as if avenging Severino hinges on this. If Sevi cannot be made to yield, Attorney Sandoval can find a way, must find the way. Sons do not need to inherit everything. Telly is Severino's favorite niece. The house can go to her. Though she will probably find a way of turning it into something useless.

The bedroom door is opened and closed. It is too quick for Maria Esperanza to catch what she hears. It makes her feel as if she is in her casket and someone has opened the lid to look inside. She shivers and closes her eyes. Opens them immediately again. Severino is seven years younger than she, she should not have outlived him. I want to die, too, she prays; not wishing to wake her sisters up or to be left alone. The scent grows. She pushes her legs out of the bed. Once and for all it is time to see if it is Severino in his casket. She reaches for her cane, brushes it aside in the dark. Its falling wakes up the other two.

''What is it?'' they ask.

''Nothing,'' Maria Esperanza answers. They'll think she is crazy. They'll insist it is Severino's body the men brought up and start arguing about whether there were six or eight men. She knows there were eight and pulls her legs back into bed. In the morning she will send for her son who is the general and tell him to do something. People disappear, but not her brother.

Even this decision fails to make her fall asleep. It continues to weigh in her mind, that fear which began with the odor. All the possibilities she has considered come in full force to her. She names the culprits in her mind, absolves and indicts them again with all the intensity of those who can no longer make things happen. And of the many things that occur to her, one remains upon which she dwells. Concerning Telly, she wakes up her sisters, with her idea. "We should have a wedding. It is lucky to have a wedding follow a wake."

The other two murmur their replies, but Maria Esperanza does not intend to have them tell her anything. Her own inclinations are what she declares: to have Telly remarry Quiel, have Sevi celebrate it in his church. "It is the only way to heal the breach perfectly," she says, thinking of whom to summon in the morning in order to initiate the proper approaches. "It can be while the Pope is here."

In rearranging lives, Maria Esperanza will not be opposed.

# BOOK TWO: Wednesday

# 1

Don Severino's sisters wake up at different times in his house and are served their first breakfast by their own servants who have also slept in that house and discovered from the servants there that Don Severino had not been home for weeks.

The sisters warn their servants to say nothing of this to anyone else while they try to figure out its significance. At different stages of breakfast, they watch one another eat. Maria Esperanza breaks up a *pan de sal* into a wide cup of chocolate, stirs the pieces with a teaspoon. "Clearly, he has another home elsewhere."

"Mamá used to say of Papá, 'Face him in any direction and he has slept there.'" Maria Paz decides to ask for another *estrellado*. The rest of the day all she will have is soup into which whole eggs have been beaten; and cola into which raw eggs are stirred. Uncooked eggs are her main nourishment, for she cannot chew with her gums and she refuses to have false teeth for fear of swallowing them.

"It would have helped if Severino had gone to worship those in Malacanang as others did," Maria Caridad discloses her preoccupation with being in good standing with governments. "But, I think he's right. Papá used to say, 'If God does not force me to kneel before Him, should I let a mere man, even if he is president or governor?' Severino never refused God, though. He knelt long hours on Fridays at Quiapo and on Tuesdays before the Virgin of the Pillar in Santa Cruz. He sent donations to every priest who asked for it. And he did many other works of charity for God. The only one he would not gladly give was Sevi. But we all, each of us in the world, have an Isaac God asks us to give up. I still think that if Severino had raised the boy himself, he could have talked him out of the priesthood. They took turns loving each other. That was the problem. If only people loved one another at the same time, they would do anything for each other. *Kung magkalihis*, if they slip past..."

The other two sisters listen to Maria Caridad in surprise that she has enough breath in her body for such a long speech. Seeing their surprise, she draws their attention away from her by looking towards the altar, and sees Sevi standing there. "Is that Sevi saying Mass?"

Maria Esperanza fixes her eyes upon Sevi, able to see only his large movements. "We'd better sit at the altar. Did you hear him call? He should have let us know he would say Mass this early. Who will celebrate it tonight when there will be more people?" She calls the servants from the kitchen, tells the children to gather forward. "Everyone kneel. There's room there. You. You move closer to the casket. Why, are you afraid? Drop on your knees and start praying immediately. Stop whispering." Maria Esperanza brings the hall to silence. Her need to give orders is as incurable as anger.

Sevi lifts his head up from prayer, sees his aunts taking their places before the altar, assembling all the others. Trying to unite his thoughts with Christ's, Sevi looks over their heads towards the wall where the lights are reflected halfway up the wood. He cannot raise their souls in prayer if he will be distracted by their voices. He drops his eyes among the flowers covering his father's casket, waiting to be possessed once more with prayer so he can mix water and wine in the chalice, the symbols of the man/God mystery, the fusion of Creator and the created: the gifts offered to the Father and returned by Him to the faithful at the Eucharist.

"He is angry," Maria Esperanza whispers to each of her sisters, telling them, "Severino closes his eyes, too, when he's angry. But why should he say Mass so early, as if he wants to say it to himself?'' She looks about her, placing a finger across her lips so Sevi, glancing up, will notice her quieting the children.

That sense of intimacy with Christ's own priesthood comes to Sevi through sacramental grace after his will fails, and he leads them to prayer by praying, his thoughts with Christ who bore human pain, who continues His agony in order to accompany ours, in fulfillment of His promise to be with us. He tells them that God calls everyone, not only saints, to the vocation of holiness.

Maria Esperanza cries as the words reach her: The greatest sin is hopelessness. She beats her chest and remains kneeling after the others get up. The others wonder what upset her and are confused when Maria Esperanza looks up and cries, ''I have sinned.'' Her sisters cannot believe what they hear.

Sevi starts leaving before he can be offered breakfast. He feels rejected by the irreverence with which his relatives take part in the Mass. At the top of the stairs he meets more relatives coming up. He makes way for them without introducing himself. At the lower door he realizes, too late, that they will consider him arrogant for not greeting them.

''Father Sevi,'' a servant runs after him, out in the sidewalk. ''They are asking for you to come back.''

The breathlessness of the summons takes Sevi by surprise, but he turns around without asking why. It is only that Maria Esperanza wants to confess; right then to tell him about her life of sinfulness. But she cannot speak. The words are gasps of air. Several glasses of water are brought forward, Maria Esperanza refusing them in succession, motioning everyone away. He drops on his knees so she can confess.

Sevi places an arm about his aunt. The stiff *panuelo* pricks his sleeve. She appears to be as much disturbed as someone who has come to confess having killed another: ''I did not want to do it, Father, but something moved my hand''; or someone summoning him in the middle of the night to bless

77

a dying parent, a stricken child: waiting for him to say something by which life can be understood and endured. It is among those in grief that his love is dispersed, for he feels just as abandoned as they are. In this lies his absolute freedom to love only God. Absolving her, he looks up at the crucifix. Then rising, Sevi Gil bends down over his aunt, his cassock a white cave over her mourning clothes. "Aunt, God loves those He created. In order to be saved, it is enough to believe in the good news that God wants us to be happy with him in heaven where we will live as long as He. There is nothing He will not forgive us..."

This is not what Maria Esperanza needs to hear. Her pride demands that she be singled out for special anger from God, for a punishment reserved alone for her. She wants that; and then to see the heavens open and angels to descend. It is farthest from her desire to be loved along with everyone else, to be saved with others. So she cries harder on being told that she is included, with all the rest, in God's plans.

Relatives cluster around in order to hear what is being exchanged between them. Maria Esperanza is revived by their attention and she insists on introducing Sevi herself, is extremely delighted when he obediently follows her about the hall. Jaime, her son who is a priest, will not indulge her this way, will not be petted in front of others. She is soon lapsing into memories only she can follow, prolonging introductions in order to keep Sevi beside her.

Sevi suffers the introductions. Even from the beginning, all he wanted was a life of contemplation as a way of sharing God's happiness and thoughts. The silence of a monastery was better suited to his nature. There, nothing could inflame his anger, which can be a terrible thing, fed by his feelings of abandonment by his father. Only when it became quite clear that the perfection of monasticism was too easy, did he decide to renounce himself totally while remaining in the world where he could be wounded and challenged, where the constancy of his faith was not something he could accomplish once and for all, where he would have to decide, again and again, which comes first: total commitment to God or total commitment to man, to discover where they coincide.

Standing in his father's house quickly becomes one of those times when he cannot feel God. He has been deprived of that consolation time and again before, but he wants it especially during his father's wake. Some other time he can live in the desert – and what better desert than a crowded slum? – but right now he wants to be stunned by God's love, by God's knowing him by name. When God feels this remote from him, Sevi cannot even pray. He succumbs to anger that the One he calls Father, after his own rejected him, will deliberately withhold Himself. It is a nightmare, a darkness even though he realizes that only thus can he reach a point where the consolation of God's presence ceases to be the overriding desire, when God becomes the One who is sought.

God who desires us even more than we desire You: Sevi tries to pray while around him people continue to talk. Their words burst and ricochet, travel like gunfire, repeat like musical compositions springing into surges and figurations that tease the ear. Here are relatives from Tarlac, from Bicol and Antique; from Pangasinan, Batangas and Laguna; from all the provinces to which the Gils have scattered, intermarried and returned; each one speaking in the accent and pattern of his region, totally appealing and charming in diversity which, in point of sound, makes of the wake something of a high festival with the flowers entirely covering the casket and reaching up to the altar like medallions.

In this family, he thinks, one has to be beautiful, or rich, or close to those in power, or all of these preferably, in order to be admired. The walls frame the faces that are startlingly similar in the eyes and the mouth. He has never seen all of his father's family gathered together, and he wishes to hide from them, for he feels he is on trial even when they are talking of everything else but him.

They are talking about Gaddafi and the Moslem Liberation

Front, about what had been heard of his giving Aquino money to sustain a 20,000 man force in Borneo, of the old tiger Taruc delivering Marcos' messages to exiles in America. One uncle's interest is on the boat people of Vietnam. "Aren't we boat people, too, in a manner of speaking?" The talk goes back to the Japanese Occupation. An uncle recalls that he and others had been brought out of Fort Santiago, lined up along the banks of the Pasig where gasoline was poured over them. Before he could be set on fire with the others, he leaped into the river. "The torch was just inches from my arm. Now, they're all over the city. Our college girls ... Well, you know, they pay top price for flesh. So, we're red-light district for Asia."

"Before the war a forty-five peso clerk wouldn't sell his soul for any bribe. But corruption is one way of dividing the spoils," an uncle turns to the cousin whose wife and sons are waiting for him in Hong Kong so they can proceed from there to Canada. "How long will you be away? At least you can read a newspaper that has news, real news."

"Until the government is changed. I can't take it any more. I'm governor of my province, you know. I have to defend the government or be sent to indoctrination school. But how can I keep leading the celebration of Besang Pass in place of Corregidor, Thanksgiving on the day martial law was declared? I've heard there was no Besang Pass to speak of. I have to appear on TV praising the administration for the prosperity it has brought to the country when none of it has found its way to my province. I have to pledge allegiance to the President instead of to the country, so I cannot talk against the sintering plant Kawasaki built in Mindanao. In the industrially polluted parts of Brazil, children are being born without brains ... Respiratory ailments and deformities have already appeared in our region. And the destruction is irreversible. We accepted this plant, which the Japanese will not allow in their country, as part of Japanese economic aid. Of the 29,000 people displaced by the plant only 75 were hired.

We have lost our economic and political sovereignty to the administrators of martial law who allow these things . . . ''

''What you say is true. We're thinking of going to New Jersey. What convinced my wife is the time she was in Malacanang and Madame came out in a long white gown reminiscent of the Virgin. Double lines of little girls dressed as angels ushered her out to trumpet blasts. She expects worship. And for the President's birthday, didn't you hear? She has commissioned a book affordable only by the super-rich. It is to be called *Si Malakas at Si Maganda: The Strong and the Beautiful, The Legend of Creation*. Title roles in history and in religion,'' another confirms.

The governor smiles ruefully. ''Our clothes are still hanging in the wardrobe, so no one will suspect. Friends in the tourism office took care of our passports. At Customs, a friend is prepared to state, should I be questioned, that I am on a mission for the government. People still try to help one another at least. So, we might not see each other for some time, Father; I might not be able to come for my parents' wake. But if the extradition treaty with America passes . . . ''

Sevi feels some kind of assurance is expected from him, but he does not know what and he feels uncomfortable.

A ninety-year-old uncle attempts to console him. ''Your father was a good man. Virtues are not needed to survive; in fact, only bring disaster. But your father kept his. Oppression can be endured; poverty can be borne. They're not of our making. But the loss of virtues is the death of a man. It's all wilderness now, as far as I can see. An old man is saying this to you, a priest. But I'm old enough to have seen God relenting, opening the gate of peace, then closing it again. Perhaps we cannot bear too much of it.''

''Perhaps, Uncle,'' Sevi replies, restless in his father's house.

''So, you're his son. We talked about you. He was proud of you when you stood up to him. Not many have. I'll tell you . . . he also wanted to be a priest. When we were young and everything seemed possible, we all wanted to become priests. But we could only be ordinary men, trading off our ideals for pleasure, for prosperity.'' The old one drew close to the casket. ''Sealed! What a good idea.''

''He wanted it.''

''Tell me, it's true is it not, that God allows sin and evil in the world so we can choose to deserve heaven instead of hell? He hopes we'll choose Him, does He not? I've always thought He uses our weakness to make us long for Him. He and I, God, have had very long conversations. One of these was when my wife was dying. It took such a long time. She could no longer talk. You see, she had cancer of the throat. I talked to her through Him. God was patient. He stayed with me throughout. So, everything, if we live long enough, brings us back to Him, does it not? So Severino wanted a sealed casket.''

Sevi refrains from telling his uncle that a woman whose voice he did not recognize called him on the phone to tell him his father had been brought to what used to be the Mary Johnston Clinic. Heart failure. She did not sound as if she had been crying. When he got there his father had been moved to the morgue. At the morgue, he arrived too late to see his father. The casket had already been nailed shut. It came to him as he stood among the unclaimed bodies that he had no right to judge his father or question his wish since a person's faith and state of grace is known only to God.

Sevi stands before the coffin feeling nothing. It is like experiencing the absence of God after having been comforted by His presence. The more one desires to feel Him, the more He seems remote. He dismisses his need as a vain desire to be the chosen one of God.

They are asking him questions about his father by way of seeing where he stands on the issues dividing them. Avoiding politics for fear it will lead him away from God, he does not respond to their efforts. He knows though that it has become increasingly monstrous, having to be careful about what one says even among friends, but he considers it enough that he is a priest. He knows, however, of priests who are revolutionaries. Unless he has crossed into Mindanao, a cousin of his who is a Jesuit is with the NPAs in Samar. This cousin wrote poems while in college, is the last person anyone would expect to practise the theology of liberation directly. But contemplation in action is this man's kind of mysticism, his way of taking political and social responsibility in keeping with his vows of obedience. Freedom in obedience, life in death can center one's life and purpose in Christ. But civil war will be fought over the bodies of the people, who will be brutally ''salvaged'' or ''liberated'', according to which side did the killing.

More relatives are coming up, for the first time that second morning of the wake. There is no way for Sevi to attach names to faces. The moment he thinks he has his relatives identified, they move aside and mingle, become confused with someone else. Each new mourner seems to add to the darkness of the house which has become as sad as an old church where the Mother of Sorrows is enshrined, provided with a delicately embroidered handkerchief to catch the enameled tears on its face. The dark clothes merge with the walls. Only the flash of diamond on ears and necks, the glint of gold, relieve the eyes.

Sister Lutgarda comes up, bringing some of her students, who scatter among their classmates in the hall. Maria Esperanza welcomes them, orders the table to be set for them. Sister Lut, as she is called, makes a round of the relatives. She is sixty-five but looks about twenty years younger, almost like a ''bride adorned in readiness'', for her face is bright, shiny with joy. God's love seems to keep her lively.

''Sister, are you still in sex education?'' Finina asks, expecting others to catch the combination: a nun and sex.

''What do you know about sex, Sister Lut?''

Sister Lutgarda holds the cup of hot chocolate in the air and delays her reply, until everyone has said something on the subject. Then, while her students and their classmates go off to one corner to sing the Maryknoll version of *Makibaka/ Huwág matakot*, ''Fight Back, Have Courage'', one of the marching songs of the demonstrations, she answers them, ''Of the physical part of sex, I know only what reason and common sense allow me to deduce, but I know that it is ignorance of sex that causes people to abuse one another. Sex can be beautiful. The Bible speaks of the love between man and woman in the same way as God's love for us. Sex with love can help us grow towards God. Come to our workshops. I am trying to bring sex education to the home with pilot projects. Sex is part of family life, part of commitment beyond loyalty.''

Maria Esperanza sends Maria Caridad to her daughter. ''Ask her to lead the rosary. I will have no more talk about *malicia* while Severino is lying in state. Nuns are supposed to spend their days in prayer, and look holy.'' By this she means suffering. That is the sign she expects God's presence to take. She throws Aurelio Gil a disapproving look when he gets up to say that nuns are the bravest men in the Philippines, because there are four of them to every priest who stands up to the government. Maria Esperanza thinks that Sister Lut should have been kept in the Missions in Mindanao instead of being allowed to spread her gospel about sex education in Manila. She refuses to admit a sex-oriented, sex-saturated society inevitably sanctions infidelities through *queridas*. ''Tell her to lead the rosary and tell her students to stop singing.''

His aunt's annoyance disturbs Sevi, who, watching Sister Lut, is somehow reminded of the mystic-saint of the Cistercian order who had a stigmata on her side, a flowing wound like Jesus. His thoughts are interrupted by an elegantly dressed woman, another cousin he supposes, who stands in front of him. Long fine fingers hold his arm. What an exquisite form, his father would have said. She says something which he does not hear. She is staring into his face and her perfume floats above the scent of drying flowers. It is a beautiful face, demanding admiration.

He forces his thoughts back upon the governor. Could he have said something that would have made a difference to his cousin? Not many absorb being told that God is faithful to man and will be with him to the end of the world. The world ended again and again for man; ended with lifetimes. What difference would it have made if he had been able to say that Jesus came in history, will come at the end of the world but that his second coming – into the present – is a fact that does not have to be held in faith alone. Hidden in immaculacy how can he be the one in whom God is encountered? Yet if he succumbs to the world, how can his life be an argument for belief in the kingdom yet to come?

The fine loop of gold on the woman's neck is like lace, a transparent leaf shaking the light. He turns away in his mind by telling himself she is one of those who seek luxurious and excellent dangers into which to escape from boredom. If there are such as she, can life be said to consist only of suffering? Can an unbroken heart have anything to offer God?

He moves back towards the altar and she moves alongside him. His father, careless of his young ears, once said that too wide a band of lace in a woman's underwear classifies her as déclassé. "Like too loud perfume!" The room is vibrating finely. Sevi looks about for a place where it stands still, where he can suffer silence and meet himself.

Sevi is introduced to Sol, one of the President's friends. "Just tell him what you need and he'll get it for you. Name the park in front of your church after Imelda and you will get a cathedral, something of the kind." Sevi learns that Sol got a loan for a clay factory which failed almost as soon as imported machines to make tiles were set up, so that Sol ended up with a large Swiss account. The fact seems to be a matter of pride. Aurelio Gil remarks that since it has become progressive to cheat, to live at the expense of the country and future generations, the most endangered species in the country has to be the conscience-torn, honor-bound man.

"Have you always wanted to be a priest?" the beautiful

cousin finally speaks words he can understand.

But Sevi is not certain what she expects to hear. If God really wanted someone, there is no place to hide oneself. He believes he has answered the call out of his own weakness, out of the need to call someone father; but he suspects he has not remained selfish, for there are times when he feels Christ living fully in him. Yet there are also times when his self-emptying, to give Christ room, is pure spitefulness. What strange dwelling places the Lord takes!

The woman is looking at him, bringing her face up to his, as if to eat the words right out of his mouth, and he is angry that God will allow him to be tempted this way; and during his father's wake. Make me faithful, he calls back; make me faithful in the line of Melchisedech. He calls to the God who might not be listening; who might not exist. This anger is the place of his exile, of his fear and of his loneliness: a place as dark as death. He has wrestled with it enough times to know it also provides him with the sense of risk that quickens life. Controlling it has, time and again, led him to a feeling of peacefulness; but while it reigns in him, he is wrecked.

Make me faithful, he prays. Do not allow my faith to be reduced to rituals that allow my mind to rest elsewhere. Is it a failure of his faith to find his thoughts sometimes distant from God? Is it because he has never felt loved that he can love only intermittently and from a distance; that he cannot respond to the sufferings of his relatives?

Someone is saying goodbye to him, pressing his arm. As he turns sideways, he sees his face in the mirror. Immediately, he looks away. The mirror tells him he is nothing to admire, and yet his father's relatives seek him in his father's house. Here is another uncle, who reaches up only to his shoulders so that he has to bend over in order to hear the words being said to him, ''Don't think too harshly of your father. The last months of his life he was doing something to make up for all the years he obeyed only the laws of his body. We are wretched creatures, as you know. The allurements of sin so easily slay us . . . ''

Free me from myself, Sevi prays, wanting to look ahead to the Pope's coming as a prefigurement of salvation, for this to accompany his own incarnation. Christ is somehow resurrected in some men, crucified in others. He does not know which he is.

His need to feel God constantly can only be an immature need for manifestation, a high conceit. Encumbered fully with his feelings, how is he different from those who, in order to escape the demands of knowing, choose to know *about* God instead of *knowing* Him?

The sun has come up fully upon the second day of the wake. Ashamed of his easily aroused emotions, Sevi sees the hall as a place where things have fallen from where they have stood.

# 2

Telly wakes up thinking: Some die early and often; which sounds like the absolute truth, so she thinks it again until like a strange plant, the thought blooms inside her. She falls asleep, wakes up with it wreathing her bones. His paws on her bed, Henry looks at her, as if he can see her thought.

It's noon when she wakes up fully, too late to drive up to Baguio. Falling asleep the night before, she thought of driving to the mountains, five-six hours going, another five-six returning just to be able to look down on the green lake that had been formed by a landslide, to watch the dead green waters rising on the trunks of the pine trees along the riverbed that had been spliced by the falling earth. Above the pines, the clouds were always fatter than bodies asleep.

She would have changed her mind at the last minute, she tells herself. She might not have gone at all even if she had not slept the day away; not gone anywhere. Without someone, someone desired, to share the new lake, it would not be worth the effort. "Someone to be enchanted with," she speaks, as if explaining herself to another. Henry lays his paws on the tiled floor of the *azotea*, pulling them away so gently that the sheets are not displaced a bit. Assured by her voice, he lays his head on his paws and blinks at Telly.

She sits up in bed. The shelter of leaves also keeps away the heat and Telly lifts up both arms to stretch. Her wrists are sore as if they have been held tight and only then released. It could be poor circulation, she warns herself, recalling what her doctor in Katonah said about no longer being programmed to survive after forty-five. How long one lives afterwards depends upon how well one takes care of oneself. Well, she is forty-nine, but she will never take the time to stay alive. I can die any time, she says; I'm not afraid. I'll merely walk into the sky . . .

Though she wants to die, she lives. Her doctor asked, pressing her, "Have you always wanted to die? Was it only after you discovered that husbands come and go?" She shakes the question off now by rising, deliberately refusing to stretch through the exercises devised to tone up the body, to make it feel alive. Eleven months she grappled with the question in the Unit, asked it of herself, asked by all the therapists and psychologists who walked through her life in the hospital. She never gave an answer. Close to the end of winter, with the peach trees still glazed in buds, she signed herself out of the hospital without waiting for medical advice. That time she had no wedding ring to leave behind to mark something ended. Yet, she feels now that she left a friend, perhaps the only one she ever will have. She feels she can still call her doctor and pick up from the last word they exchanged, unless he is dead or old, which is the same as dead. He said the Unit is the 20th-century monastery.

Now her ankles are sore, too, along with her wrists. She decides to leave the soreness at home. In front of her wardrobe, Henry positioned to the side, watching/guarding, she changes several times, always displeased by something she cannot put her finger on. Nothing is ever right. The clothes feel like leaves and feathers with strange scents, like the herbs her uncle Aurelio Gil prescribed. She remembers him giving her ten centimos if she would take the spoonful of cod liver oil with raw sugar scraped into it.

She tries on different shoes and leaves unmatched pairs about her bedroom; leaves them looking like strange footsteps belonging to those who might have been pulled up into the air. Is that the way one dies? she wonders, picking up a dress from those she had dropped on the floor, thrown on the bed.

Regardless of what people think, is that the way one actually dies?

I can drive down to Tagaytay instead, Telly juggles plans in her mind. Perhaps walk down to the lake within the lake, a crater of water. Why water, all of a sudden? She shivers from the cold of the river in Katonah, of all the rivers she has walked into in the States. Why do I want to see water and from a height?

She takes her old Kharman Ghia up and down Recto, unable to decide if she will go into her uncle's house. He doesn't care, she thinks; no one in that house cares if she has no one now, no one who will stop whatever he is doing or thinking to talk to her. Even when he was winning at monte, her uncle came. Even when he could not see her thoughts, he took the time to hold her and tell her to be patient. "When we're ready for it, what we want will happen." She passes the house another time. Is it happening, what I want? she asks. No one she recognizes is at the windows. No one who sees her passing below, waiting to be asked to come up, to be pleaded with. He does not look like his father at all. Another time she passes the house and still he has not looked out. She feels imperfect, capable of hate.

Her doctor said that hurt and anger are two different emotions. One gets over anger but the hurt stays, can become one's principal self; the one who cannot be endured. He said that she might not have been trying to end her life when she walked into the river. "It could be that you were at the end of your resources as a person, that you wanted to get rid of a part of the past so you could live without its memory."

On the sidewalk there are still wreaths waiting to be brought up. They stand farther apart now. The day before, they stood against each other, a line of mourners.

Passing the house, she strains for a glance back as if expecting to see the grey car in the driveway of *piedra china*. That was always the sign that her Uncle Severino was home. He was never home very long, was always in and out like a visitor.

She has not needed to see him for months. Had he needed her? Was talking to her something he looked forward to, a part of his life he would prefer to keep doing? Perhaps he needed her finally and she was not available to him. We are all strangers, myself most of all, she thinks.

On the sidewalk, a small golden shower tree is dropping its leaves, making Telly think of inverted fountains. The air hangs over the tree like a crown.

She looks back at the curtains blowing at the windows before racing towards Dulong Bayan and Divisoria, towards Plaza Moriones from there, towards the wharf where instead of the sea, one smells old floods caught in the street canals, held hostage for the dry season. In the middle of the day it feels to her that the sky is full of black stars blowing. The roofs of buildings and row houses are ridges claimed by moonbreak. Houses with falling shutters and sagging walls are full of old women and of children wearing old clothes which make them look like rags drying upon fences, and the grimmer fairytales in jars of foetuses preserved in formaldehyde.

New housing, which the really poor cannot afford to rent although this has been announced for them – BLISS homes – remind Telly of bundled firewood. The tight walls are sterile trees in a condemned city where at the end of the road that accompanies the shore there will be huts huddled over piles of garbage, people living on top of the source of their living. Once she caught sight of a red-haired man wearing jockey shorts like the other residents and she passed by several times later, hoping to be certain but was distracted by the *bancas* sitting on the water of the fishponds that will all soon be filled up for more housing. She stopped at the edge of the road, watching the *bancas*, the weight of the single men riding them pushing one end into the dark waters and lifting the other to the sky, the outline of a wing, a thrust leg of an insect. It changed the significance of life somehow to have it managed. That part of the city is turned into a heartless forest. No birds are singing inside the bushes.

She looks back through the rearview mirror. Ever since she left Quiel, for twenty-nine years, she has felt watched and followed. Some times, it bothered her. Often she merely felt accompanied. Once, she somehow had the idea it was God; of all the mad ideas that occurred to her, why that? And she turned around and said, What do you want? As if God spoke. Then she ran to her uncle to tell him how it was. He was listening to her strangely, one eye fixed staring, the other asleep; though both were open.

Because where she finds herself is not where she wants to be, she turns against the traffic, causing a screeching of brakes and curses into which she turns again because it occurs to her that if she went on where she was headed she might see Father Sevi's church. She imagines he will be surprised. And if he does not recognize me, so much the better. So clever seems the idea that she has driven some length along Juan Luna before she realizes she does not know which one is his church – slums stretch out in all directions behind the houses along the road, lengthening like mimosa on the dikes of rice-fields; and he might be back in the house on Recto.

However, she is only momentarily perplexed. Her way to a decision is to keep on going until she stumbles upon it, confident some sure and perfect knowledge will come upon her on the way. This time she is impatient. She counts the moments as if they are being wasted by the simple fact of their passing. Landmarks recall the times she has visited, on this road, people who used to live there. It all amounts to nothing, she thinks, all those visits which cannot stop lives from ending. I have been an attempted child/I have never/Become. Have I ever visited myself?

The sudden screeching of brakes cuts off her thoughts. Like sunlight disturbed upon a pond the street breaks up into people running into the sun and back into the sidewalks. A child is trying to rise. She sees its head and then its arms. It stands up halting, runs, stands up still then, its whole body limping, disappears into the crowd of people, against whose bodies she sees the child who has disappeared, sees it stand almost straight, look at her and then away, as if driven by shame or guilt, racing into the alley from which more people are coming to stop just ahead of her car as if at a barrier she cannot see. The light divides them.

It is strange, she thinks, to be seeing what I have seen, to see it beyond my seeing. Like fine rain the sunlight stops, hangs in the air. On the road it forms reverse ripples returning the dry edges to the circling center, puddles of light trying to catch the fugitive sun overhead.

Telly gets out of her car, does not close the door after her or take the key off the ignition, acting against all instincts to be cautious. She looks where the people are staring. There is nothing there but a pair of blue rubber slippers, flung apart. The size could fit any child, but she is certain it belongs to the one who fled into the crowd. "She ran over him," someone accuses. Telly looks up quickly with anger. Another says, "No, he ran into her car."

The people are arguing. The idea of being the subject of their interest appalls Telly, even more than the accusation, for she certainly did not feel the car hit anyone. Dare these strangers walk at will into her life, try to decide what she has done or has not done? Although her earliest and most enduring lessons are in courtesy and in restraint, she picks up her heels and turns away abruptly, dismissing them. But the people are at her shoulders, pressing at her.

How she dislikes people who come uninvited to her life, wandering at will in her thoughts. All she needs is a friend who is no one else's friend, who will allow her moments of silence and sudden cheerfulness that is not a response to any person or occasion, but is itself. But the one she thinks can be this friend loves no one separately, must love everyone purely. Where is the specialness she requires, the absence of limits to the friendship? Has she lost that chance to the medications prescribed for her in Katonah, like the woman who kept crying at everyone who came that she had just lost her child to the pills prescribed for her depression.

I give my child her dead mother, Telly thinks, trying to sort out her instincts which tell her to return to the safety of her car. Precisely because it is safe, she hesitates before she obeys.

She turns the key in the ignition, forgetting she has not turned it off. The engine shrieks. She races ahead. Pressing jeepneys and cars and trucks and buses forward. Wondering from where the future is coming, she forgets to look for Sevi's church.

Past Navotas she finds herself, pushed ahead by a sudden headache. A brightly plumaged bird she calls the pain, angry at herself for reacting to stress as if she knew no better. It is a danger signal, this turning of anger on herself. It happens because she is the one most available to herself, the one against whom she can most easily strike. The one she can slay without feelings of guilt.

By recalling what she knows of trees, she tries to lead herself away from the anger that proceeds from the accident. There is first of all the bark, then the sapwood, then the dead heart preserved around a thin bark. Death of feeling preserves the wound through which anger cannot rise. You're tricking yourself, she warns. You're giving yourself mixed signals so you can do what you please. There is no reason to trust what you think or feel. There is no reason to trust. The anger is a small but confident pain, her body remembering.

"Don't mislead yourself," her doctor told her twenty-five years ago. That long? Where did the years go? She was barely twenty-five, four then. He said she was tougher than a spider web. "You can put yourself together again but first, you have to be convinced you want to do it."

She resented not having an odd deviant distress impossible to diagnose; felt challenged to be told that she was resisting medication. Treatments, shock or drugs, worked the reverse with her. She retained what was supposed to be erased from her mind: Quiel's unfaithfulness. Splice my brain, she asked them. Cut off the hurt, she answered the psychologist testing

94

her reactions. Very early on, they stopped astonishing her with what they called discoveries. She did not want to be surprised because she did not want to be alive.

She has put herself together, though not too well, so it will not take too much of an effort to die. Though to have come that far so well, her doctor said, she had to be strong. They surprised each other with their strength. Taking leave of him, she told him that she did not think she would try to kill herself again. He said, ''I take that as a statement of your intention, not as a promise.'' Was he looking ahead then, trying to free her to her own will? ''If only I have a reason not to die,'' she said. ''Do you believe in God?''

He said, ''Without a creator, what we know of our world and of the universe remains just elegant facts. Nothing more.'' But more he added: that writing was a way of being present in the world. He thought it was a far more courageous thing than managing someone's midnight heart attack. Why did he not say yes or no? for her sake, lie, if necessary? He said though that he would think of her. From time to time she thinks of him, misses him. He helped her by wishing to be of help. They both liked Monet, were both devoutly skeptical.

Thinking of surprising Sevi in his church is the first clear and vibrant feeling she has had in years. It feels like the sun on her face in the dead of winter.

Her thoughts circle. She keeps seeing the boy fall under her car, not from having seen it happen but from surmising, from having seen him trying to rise; keeps feeling the people wrapping themselves about her, pushing her against the boy running into the doorless alley. Her thoughts become ripples, growing smaller, returning to the stone that disturbed them. She thinks of the day that Quiel left. She was twenty, a bride. By turns she sees herself a beautiful child with ribbons in her braids, then one growing full of hurt, caught in mid-air, resisting. People say she left him . . .

In the hospital at Katonah she felt invented, one being imagined, a glass without silvering. All she remembers of the milieu therapists are mouths and voices bouncing off her face; luxurious and mechanical sounds trying to find out secrets about her. She talked only to the doctor who revived her from drowning, who came to see her from time to time on visits that were neither entirely social nor formal either, but in between as he described, and certainly not for payment. They talked about writing, how he himself was writing a long story, slowly. She wonders if he ever finished it, if it remains the wish that sustains him as he manages other people's strokes and broken limbs; if he still believes that life is sustained by acts of courage, usually small acts defending dignities. He thought she was stronger than she or other people gave her credit for.

She tries to stop memory but sees more clearly infidelities and white uniforms: a self-perpetuating wake for the self. In the hospital they told her what she did wrong, but not what she could do right because each person is supposed to be an *only* person to whom different rules apply. Attempting to find the rules that applied to her, she would go up to the medical section – against all regulations – to watch people being kept alive by machines. She never discovered why she kept trying to die when those close to death were trying to live.

Returning to the months she spent in Katonah's hospital is a way of wrestling with that part of her past she wants to get rid of; she wants to stop. She can still see very clearly, as if it is in her mind, the medical form with her name typed on it, and: OD. Overdose? She still gags on the pills prescribed for her so she would not then or now try to sleepwalk into the river. The first days were all unclear. It was as if she was asleep in a hammock from which she could not lift herself. One doctor, who was Czech, she trusted immediately because he was also a displaced person, he by the Russians who drove his family into exile; she by Quiel's infidelities, which keep multiplying with memory until they begin with her birth, and last beyond her dying. Infidelity sounds like a name, she thinks: infiel, infidel. She never knew if that doctor liked trees. She cannot recall him clearly through twenty-five years. When she thinks of him now, at once she sees the trees in the Plantem Garten in Hamburg, the large horses pulling beer carriages.

She orders distance and finds herself enclosed. The mind is enough space sometimes. She calls herself the deserting woman, the deserted woman by turns. Sometimes, during the day she feels silky, about to bloom and flow; then at night, she turns into the bark of trees.

The sky seen between the clouds reminds her of Sevi. The night before, during the Mass she felt something significant and new had happened, something announced and at once fulfilled. What it was, she does not have the slightest idea, only that it came upon her when they happened to look up at the same time, he from the chalice and she from herself. It passed quickly; yet when she recalls it, she feels some kind of promise has exchanged, a pledge of constancy; not human love, she thinks; not something imperfect and halting and unjust, but something between people who count in each other's lives, even if only for a moment. Soulmates, perhaps.

She refuses to allow herself such long thoughts about Sevi and wills memory elsewhere to other men. The young marine talked of four-hour highs after she had watched him land his helicopter on the American Embassy ground at Dewey, ten minutes from Subic by air. His colonel recognized her from some reception but was on his way to the briefing for joint maneuvers in the South China Sea, so she, having come from the cafeteria which she thought served the best french fries in Manila, got to talk to his aide, while he waited for the colonel. She liked the uncomplicated way the young marine thought of her. ''Hey, ever been in Marin County?'' he asked, clearly not expecting to be answered in the affirmative. He was twenty-four and by his own admission already tired of philosophers like Ginsberg. ''I'm in the marines to try the real hard stuff, not a hand-me-down from Freud. You know, the shrink man.''

She pretended ignorance so he would keep talking. He

looked like mother's boy, grown up on milk and apple pie, when he tried bursting his chest that tapered down to a stiff belt and boots shined to the glow of patent leather. She looked impressed. He carried on his act by reciting poems about being cold outside but ''warm inside our stillness'', his hands at his side as if he were on parade dress. ''That's snow for you,'' he said, certain she had not seen the stuff so he proceeded to explain snow to her. ''The poem is about falling in love with the snow about one's heart.'' His right hand went up to the button nearest his heart. ''Real deep stuff, poetry.''

He asked if she ever read Mc ... somebody's poetry. ''He says things like, 'Space is all loneliness/One keeps falling out/ To single orbit.' Great stuff. It hits you right there.''

He makes a gesture like *mea culpa*. ''He says, 'Sex is a sacrament.' One poem talks about the 'whites in lovers' lies.' Real Great. I'm tough but those poems bring me close to crying. Boy. They do the work of three bottles and the hangover is good. It makes you sail real high. You should read them. I could bring it the next time. . . . ''

Inside of twenty minutes, talking to him in her black cocktail dress worn for the reception to launch Jayjay's latest book of poetry, she learns the young marine is a Methodist, that one brother, ''the one who clowned the minute he came out of my mother'', has won a singing audition in Tampa. ''You know where that is? This place here,'' he sweeps the bay area with his hand, ''sure reminds me of Tampa.''

He started her car after she flooded the engine. In gratitude, knowing he could not come, she asked him to the poetry launching.

''I'll tell you what,'' he said, ''let's do something together the next time I see the colonel to the city. You meet me right here. Let's go to Taal. You know where that is? I'll bring three Jack Daniels and you bring the grub.''

She said yes while thinking he was a child of loneliness like her. The only difference is that he ''warms his ass'' on the leather of his jeepney while she ... She refused to think it through.

"Have you seen fireflies?" he asks, his hand on the car window.

"We have fireflies," she answers. The car is idling fast and she is anxious to swing out of the parking place, for people have started to notice them.

"They're not as romantic as we might think. I read that those flying high are males looking for mates. Those on the ground are females that attract with their lights. And this is the clincher. Seventy-five per cent of those female lights on the grass are being flashed to lure the males down where they can be eaten. I mean e-a-t."

She turned off the ignition when he began to talk about his daughter and the wife who was not a mother to her . . . Some of the shock is still in her. How was she to recognize someone as fragile as herself in a body built hard enough to snub a bullet? She wonders where he is now, wonders if he ever took the trip to Taal. She forgot about it then, forgot where they were supposed to meet. She can think of Quiel and that marine only as they are/were; not embellished in wish or fantasy.

Which brings her back to Sevi, back to her desire for a god of flesh; which makes her feel sinful. Even if she never betrays her feelings to another, it would be sacrilegious, she thinks. It is sinful enough to feel happy when she sees him. For the rest of her life she is content to be happy thinking of him.

She swings to darkness, deeper. She has never been good for anyone. Not even for herself. Her thoughts persist. Why does it seem she has known him all her life when she really met Sevi only the day before? Anyway, she tells herself, protecting him, he does not know how to love. He's an inexperienced man. The important thing she must keep in mind is that she must not love. It only leads her to completely mad thoughts, bitter bewildered thoughts to which she returns willfully as to the scene of a crime. To love is to open oneself to hurt. Is that the same reason Sevi has hidden in himself? All relationships deteriorate.

Perhaps if they had known each other before Sevi decided

to become a priest ... But she would not have looked at him then. His shyness would have amused her. Yet there is stubbornness, too. His insistence on the hospice is surprising. I might have married Quiel anyway. Telly thinks. But how do I describe Sevi? Words either exaggerated or under-represented. No word is enough.

She decides to return to her Tio Severino's house, expecting to be surprised out of sadness, out of boredom, so clearly expecting something beyond astonishment even. Is it humility when he so plainly holds himself in high regard? It is in the way he stands, the way he declared he would turn the house into a hospice, as if he had rights against his father's sisters. A truly humble person would have deferred, at least during the wake; would not have stood in the center of the hall as if he knew it was his place exactly, stood before the altar among the flowers as if any minute he would throw them all out ... There are enough flowers for several gardens.

Telly knows her aunts well enough to expect they will not yield to Sevi's wishes. They have ways of waylaying Sevi in order to save him from his impulses. Perhaps I will be on his side, she thinks, though she knows that she is neither constant nor certain for very long. Possibly, it is the way of joining their lives against the others. This appeals to her greatly for she needs to risk everything. Half measures bore her. She wants to know both capitulation and victory. It is possible if one thinks of God as the one inside ourselves which we can please. It amounts, strangely, to a choice of saviors.

"There you are. You keep disappearing," Maria Esperanza greets Telly when she comes up to kiss her aunts. "Listen. I've been telling relatives we will have a wedding ... "

Right away, Telly knows whose is being planned. She sees it in the way Maria Esperanza smiles at her, and she shrinks. "It will not be mine," she announces firmly.

"*Anák*, what do you have against a wedding?" Maria Esperanza asks. "We never used to question what our parents wanted for us, child."

Maria Paz nods her head in full agreement. Maria Caridad feels she's burning. She resents Maria Esperanza's acting as if she were Telly's godmother, and she goes on to other resentments. They include her in their business deals only because it is she who brings them luck. The times they excluded her, they lost more than the capital they put in. She believes some people are lucky, some houses. Maria Esperanza is always unlucky. If she came on a picnic, it rained. If they went on a long trip, the car broke down. There is a birthmark on Maria Esperanza's neck, a mark as dark as a squashed insect.

"It's absolute obedience that the State also requires," Aurelio Gil says, smiling at Telly. "Even God does not expect that from us. He wants us to be good, He helps us to be good but He does not make us good, does He?" Aurelio turns to Sevi.

"What are laws for, then? And the ten commandments?" Maria Esperanza asks with finality. "Didn't God make us? So there."

Sevi does not say what he thinks, that the ten commandments tell people what love expects of them. They are neither threats nor impositions but form some guide to the reciprocal and free relationship between man and God, among men. He senses right away that saying this would not help Telly if she has never learned to be in control of her life, if she merely does what is expected.

"It can be my wedding only on one condition," Telly smiles impishly. "That I can choose whom I'll marry. I warn you, it is someone farthest from your minds." She turns her smile on Sevi who drops his gaze to her feet.

"Who is it?" Maria Esperanza asks, instantly resuming her vigilance over everyone in sight.

"No one here," Telly misleads them, allowing her aunts to sigh with relief for they have Quiel in mind without discussing the matter beforehand. "Do you know?" Telly asks Sevi, surprising him. She has to walk away. She feels she is about to scatter, and heads for the *azotea*. Confused by what

101

she wants of Sevi, afraid that her need of him cannot be satisfied by anything she creates, acquires or becomes, convinced that she is one of those born never to have what they want, she looks up at the *caimito* tree and tells it, "I'm happy enough, imagining happiness."

She is sought there by Susan in tight black pants. "Will you come, too?" Not bothering to explain what the invitation is about, she urges Telly, "Say yes. The cardinal is the one blessing the house. I've ordered dripless candles so we don't drop wax on the new rugs." Where it is, whose house, when, she does not say; only, "A real sauna, Telly, and a Jacuzzi built for twelve, besides the swimming pool. I've asked the three sisters, but as soon as they leave with the cardinal I'll have the place turned on for us. You'll come?"

Susan's heavy scent rubs off on Telly's arm as she releases it. It's odd, Telly thinks, answering yes. It occurs to her that people probably have God's scent on them. What is it? She fights her thoughts, knowing life can be reduced to thoughts. "Yes," she repeats, as Susan continues to cajole her after she has already agreed. "Yes," she says, looking for Sevi back in the hall, because she has thought of something to say to him, something he cannot expect. Susan pulls her out of the *azotea* to bring her into the hall. "Come and meet Sevi. He's our cousin. You can imagine how rich he'll be and will have no use for us after the funeral. What a shame he seems not to know what to do with money. He's giving the house away."

Sevi and she are introduced again and again. Every time they separate, she is brought back by the same or different relative whose mind is on other matters while performing civilities. Each time they smile as if being introduced for the first time. Perhaps he does not really remember me, Telly thinks, so she tells him, "This is the third time today..."

As if they share the same thoughts, Sevi anticipates her and answers, "Yes." He laughs but does not look at her.

She is looking away from him, thinking that he appears to be filled with energy too powerful for his body to hold in forever.

Very soon it will pour out of him, then he will look at me. Is this his appeal for her? She sees him as being careless of his life as she is of hers, so that in the sense that he did not live for himself, she assumes he wants to die. Or live with a disregard for death. Is it only power and riches that fire greed?

Here I am again, living in the extremes, Telly warns herself. Medication used to bring her back to the center, keep her in balance; then she refused to take any more. She is content being an erratic unpredictable person. I want to be my dark self. I want to be able to eat roots, if that is what occurs to me. Is she speaking for him as well? In their alikeness how can they be wills opposed? What does he want from life? Does he know, or use pretexts?

Surprisingly, she has felt calm since the wake. She could have fallen apart when she ran over the child; when she could not go to Baguio as she wished. What is making the difference? She traces her feelings back to the Mass, to her hearing Sevi pray, "We come to you, Father, with praise and thanksgiving..." Has his specialness reached her, making her feel chosen, too? And will she now stop resisting having to grow less and less in herself so God can grow in her? She is frightened. It is more comfortable to think of God only when endangered or threatened; to think that good times are owed to oneself.

Yet, Sevi does not even look at her, has turned to an uncle who is telling him that if he meets any more militant nun or priest, he is certainly going to become a Protestant and leave all his property to them.

I'll never speak to him; I'll never look at him, Telly promises. Has he ever thought of me? she wonders as she thinks back to the hospital in Katonah. Why did she wait to be in the States before making her first attempt to die? A late postgraduate being mistaken for an undergrad despite two lines below each eye, she could have lived it up. What was she chasing? She went to Europe, went to Chamonix – in a summer dress walked on the Mer de Glace, which had been formed in one of

103

the Ice Ages – rode the canals in Venice, danced in the cell Rizal might have occupied in Barcelona's Montjuich, knelt in Toledo's shrines . . . She raced to every place mentioned in the travel section of the newspapers, and reached no place. She remembers that was the time she looked dead, like a ripe fruit in the mirror. She combed her hair rarely. It matched the mad abandon of the 60's. She wore a leather visor, became a flower child in San Francisco . . .

Why is it I'm always thinking of myself in the past? She ponders this while cousins, Sevi's age, are stalking the hall like so many lions; talking about their condos, export zone regulations, weekends in European cities where sex by the week is advertised in neon over flimsy doorways. They talk as if nothing ever ended. How can Sevi stand them talking about the economy like buzzards? Nothing is going right in the country but they are prosperous. They offer to make his investments for him. They see the Pope's coming in terms of foreign correspondents and minor European aristocracy who follow celebrities like camp followers and help the administration inaugurate resorts. They speak of the poor as if they are diseased private parts that have to be excised. And they feel they are the ones oppressed because their profits are down and someone else who had nothing on his back before martial law was declared now buys P900 shirts at Rustan and rides in a Mercedes or Cadillac Seville.

Telly wants to leave but stands there, a smile fixed on her face. Any minute now someone should scream and then we can all run away. An aunt with pockmarks down the center of her face is saying flirtatiously that European women become more alluring as they age. It is with alarm that Telly realizes this is the aunt who supposedly bedded every new diplomat in town, working the embassies her own distinct way. What made her hold herself so immaculate when she had other models in their family? Her doctor wanted to know. Have you had relations before? Actual intimacies? For a while she thought he was referring to confidants.

I've had a cloistered kind of life, Telly concludes. I have been protected even from myself. She knows her wish to come alive, no longer to have to imagine herself, will never be fulfilled. Nor will she ever be able to put her past permanently aside. Everything fails sooner or later, she reminds herself. Knowing this, she has learned to let moments suffice for lifetimes. When she feels excluded, she consoles herself that it is possible to live in one's thoughts, to possess at a distance. A fragile fire surrounds her heart.

Someone with a Polaroid is calling everyone to pose. Smiles perch wide on faces, like birds with open wings. She herself smiles when her turn comes to be snapped. As her picture begins developing before her eyes, she suddenly feels cold, as if the sun is going out of the sky, becoming a harmless object. She allows the picture to leave her hands, watches instead the wind swelling the curtains. It gives the hall something of the wilderness of stars, she thinks. Against all her own expectations she waits to be introduced to Sevi again. What do I want from him? she asks herself, trying to shame herself to leave. Do I no longer want to die?

A call to *merienda* reassembles everyone at the long table where they practise courtesies like strangers. An aunt whispers into her ear, "Did I hear we will have a wedding soon?" The confidence she assumes brings Telly out of herself, forcing her face to break into color. Immediately she looks down the table and up, to serve notice on Susan, if she is sitting with them, to make no remark about hot flushes.

The two glass fruit platters make the house look like the church on Sunday, with the checks and bills upon them. Telly sits across from nieces who are dressed in ROTC uniforms. They are officers no less. She smiles at them, thinking of her time when they were sponsors, not cadets. They're probably part of the Youth group headed by one of the President's daughters, who train in Makiling, she thinks, trying not to hear the exchange between Attorney Sandoval and her Uncle Aurelio Gil, a few seats down.

Serving himself generously of the *arroz caldo*, Attorney Sandoval is seized with another original idea. "If only it were possible to elect the people. Seriously. Has anybody thought of this? We elect the president, why can't we elect the people of a country and thus weed out those who have no input? Then we'll have a damn good country to show off to the Pope. *Walang dayaan, di gaya noong panahón ng Hapon*, no, none of the corruption of the Japanese Occupation."

Aurelio Gil cannot let the remark stand. "Do you remember how we adopted the new Constitution? I live in San Juan. In January of '73 our neighborhood was called to a meeting. Just like the Japanese neighborhood associations, we were asked if we wanted rice. There were lines for rice then, you recall. Our hands went up. A photographer took pictures. The next day, there I was in the newspaper with my arm raised. The caption said, the new Constitution had been overwhelmingly approved in the barangays. That's the new election system. 'Voting' with me were youths no more than fourteen..."

"You forget our Supreme Court opined that due process had been observed. That's barangay democracy. Why do we have to follow American democracy? That's theirs. Ours is ours." Attorney Sandoval laughs. "The President will not act illegitimately. He knows his law. And the Pope...."

"The Pope will make everything right," Maria Esperanza expresses her hopes. "Life will come to normal again. I have seen each of the Popes right down to Paul, except this one. And of course the one who died within a month. I walked up the tower in Saint Peter when I was young and looked down on the Vatican gardens. It was tight going up, I couldn't turn around. I knelt before every altar in Saint Peter's and went to confession. After I see this Pope, I can die. I have no more I want." She looks as if the wind has died on her face and Telly almost goes to her, almost rises to embrace her.

Sevi's eyes feel as if ashes have blown into them. He is touched by his aunt's simple wish, as if the coming of anyone, even Jesus' coming, will make the daily struggle simple, can turn the government to one arranged in heaven, or expunge evil. Men have to want God. To want Him, and to want to be holy, which means being as human as possible. Not knowing how to reconcile himself with them, he turns to Telly and for the first time asks, ''What do you do?''

Surprised that he will speak to her after appearing to avoid her all day, she answers, ''Nothing at all. I think poems but I keep no one alive. I let the government alone. Does God expect more?'' She wishes right away that she had said something civil, and gentle; something that will lodge in his mind, with which she can be conjured.

It is a dare and a question, in its daring quite filled with hurt which Sevi does not expect from his relatives, least of all from her, for his impression of her is that of someone who has never been struck, who has not therefore learned to protect herself. But he is as wrong as those who feel that having overcome desire once, they have become strong and perfect men. And he is confused, for his thoughts do not proceed from the arrogance of one who feels himself above ordinary men. The one who is never tempted has nothing in common with Christ.

His thoughts leap from Telly to his mother. Thoughts of her occur and pass over him like a hunger that has to be satisfied again and again. Somehow he expected to meet her relatives in his father's house, expected to hear her mentioned. He thinks he remembers being held by her but there is no one to confirm this. His earliest memory is of looking up at the side window of that house and being told, ''That is your father up there.''

He had watched his father from a distance for so long that, finally, when he was asked to live in that house, he strained against being that close to him, looking back with longing to the days when he was brought up, freshly scrubbed, for Christmas and Easter and on his birthdays, to receive money in an envelope which, on returning to the hut next door, he gave up to the man and the woman who took care of him but whom he did not call mother or father, or even uncle or aunt.

What is the meaning of all that then? He remembers falling asleep inside his father's car while he visited houses at night; finally, years afterwards, being brought to be tempted to those same houses . . . A special burse for Filipino priests was established in the archdiocese of Boston. He was one of the two chosen. The announcement was the first time he realized he was part of God's plan. During the years he lived with his father in that house, all that passed between them was a handful of words, tossed back and forth like balls in a game where the rules remained yet to be established: Are you hungry? Do you need money? I won't be home tonight.

He never knew what his father felt during that long trip to Cagayan, coming down through Quezon. The trips they took seemed to have no purpose but the traveling of distances. Am I his son? He asks himself now the same question that intruded upon his thoughts at the Pater Noster. Father. Even now the word releases a distinct hurt, as sharp as an incision each time he prays it. A hurt full of guilt and also of humiliations, full of regret that he never asked the question of Don Severino Gil, never asked to be confirmed because terrified of the answer.

Now, across the hall he stands from his father's closed casket and from Telly, someone like him without a father, who used to come and leave crying, not seeing him. It now seems that large segments of their lives were one; yet they never played as children. Now she looks at him as if he makes her feel chosen, consecrated, too. What are they meant to celebrate together?

Smiling, still waiting for his answer, Telly knows firmly that she no longer wants to die.

He cannot tell if her smile is for him, if the same thoughts are passing through her mind. Only bits of her life are known to him through what relatives have said. "You should have seen her when she was twenty. A most beautiful bride." Dr. Aurelio Gil referred to a sadness in Telly. "She married a man her friends wanted to marry, only they lacked the courage to set their ambition upon him. Yet . . . the divorce was her idea.''

''You have not cried for your father,'' Telly says. ''Are you trying to be a hardhearted man?'' What she wants to know is if he is sealed with earth, too.

''You have not seen,'' he starts to say; but, afraid to be open with his feelings, he continues: ''When death is seen as a process, a journey toward the Creator, we rejoice because we realize it is life, too, during which we experience each other . . . '' Then he stops avoiding her question and answers, ''I have cried and I will cry some more. I promise you . . . '' He knows their lives are parallel.

Maria Esperanza comes between them, stands there separating them with her body. ''I have not seen you wear your mother's jewels,'' she tells her niece. ''All I see on you are large objects that look as if they have floated down the Pasig or come up during the floods. What's that?'' She looks at a heavy ivory bracelet, the color of elephant hide, avoiding having to speak to Sevi because his suggestion about the hospice reminds her of clods of earth and worms and broken skin; the loathsome end of days. She has not yet decided if she will ever forgive him and she looks angry enough that, had the cruxifix fallen at her feet, she might have walked away from it. While she stands there, waiting for Telly's answer, the light falls upon Sevi like a strong wind burning.

He would have borne Maria Esperanza's anger in order to spare Telly. He is sure they are quite the same person inside. She is full of fears her face does not betray, he thinks. She deserves unbroken promises, her own impossible perfection. He wants to tell her something but is afraid of being misjudged. Even if she laughed secretly at him, he would feel it. If the good things in her life have not led her to the Lord, who will? He looks up at the chandelier, almost fearing he has that power even as he wants it, thinking of the picture in his father's room of a young girl skipping rope. He beams as he realizes the face in that picture has just smiled at him with her eyes, past Maria Esperanza, crowning him inside with gentle thorns of longing.

# 3

I come like a fugitive, she thinks, unable to stay and unable to leave.

This time she gets as far as the stairs and no farther. Once more she returns to the drying wreaths in the *azotea*. There she can lean towards him in her heart, thinking: I want to give you something perfect/In the manner of a sealed sky/Unopened arms/Still folded dreams that will not turn to sleep/I thought I could/Until I saw you/Standing in the sanctuary of light/Looking so full of goodness/In whom the Lord is pleased/If I could know you saw me/Knew me among others/I would not need to be/Perfect.

The words make Telly wince, twist her heart. Through the single tree with leaves as shiny as buds, the sun is a fugitive too, full of tenderness in its blazing: Consumed/Flung like seeds. A poem is a place of worship, Telly thinks. In each she is on her knees, praying. But can one pray and not believe? What difference did God make if she cannot be young again, cannot be brought back to the time before Quiel's infidelities?

Even in the *azotea* she is not free from the voices in the hall. New arrivals argue the questions of the day before, with no one keeping track of what was said, by whom. Children are imputed to quite different parents each time they are introduced.

The voices halt, slip like children just beginning to walk. They are full of desperate concern: The New Society is remaking history. We will be like the rest of the world, which knows nothing about us, because we, too, will know nothing

111

about ourselves. What we know now, who will remember tomorrow? Because we cannot remember who we are, what we wanted to be, we will accept whatever happens to us, whatever is decided for us. And then we will be truly nothing. Like streets that cease to be landmarks after their names are changed repeatedly.

Telly hears the grief in the voices. But what can I do about it? she replies in her mind. If there are no truths, there must be no lies either. If history is to be rewritten, there will be no reason to remember. But memory is a burden, Telly thinks, so what if everything is decided for us? There will be no reason to think, nor to say anything; there will be no need for language for it is only necessary when we have something to say. We will need only three words/I don't know/Finally, only one/No. Or yes./Whatever is commanded.

Someone comes into the *azotea*, stopping her thoughts; she turns around. They do not greet each other, as if already they have lost their names. By staring into the ground, which has become as hard and dry as concrete, she avoids those who come out to the *azotea* for air. When they linger to talk, she brings her thoughts to the plants that used to grow there, which she recalls by their scent, not knowing their names. I have never planted anything in my life, she thinks; nothing that flowers or doesn't flower.

She brings her thoughts to her Uncle Severino of whom she knows even less than when the wake began. Will he eventually become, as he already seems to many there, just someone who died and is no longer? What did it matter then if during his lifetime people said admiringly of him, ''He is the kind of man who cannot be unseated''?

A definite poem moves strongly like waves in her mind, returns on many crests. A poem is a place of revolt. In it, we reach our strengths. She is most happy when she is thinking a poem. Then she forgets she wants to die, has wanted . . . She thinks of her doctor in Katonah, trying to recall how he stood and what he looked like twenty-five years ago.

It is possible she will not meet Sevi again after the funeral. What will remind her of him? of her recovery of desire through him? he will never know of course, must never know what she feels. Is it because she is afraid he's not strong enough in his immaculacy? Or afraid to live outside her imagination? What attracts her in the first place? Only that his life is lived simply while all of theirs, her own included, are in terrible flight, like birds not knowing where to nest.

For a while she will imagine him. This is a different kind of faithfulness. Forced to exist without an object, it will be ruled by the mind's inconstancy, its alternating heart. But why not take the risk that there is no God who demands and commands? He dares us anyway. Why not rise from a life lived in corners? She asks herself bitterly, reaching for exquisite self-control and finely apportioned feelings with which she can sleep.

Unexpectedly, the voices are happy, deep in present concerns, defeating silences.

There is nothing simple in what she feels: in a holy place but not holy, she is already jealous of the people in his church who will see him every day while she imagines him. She is angry that this fact means nothing to them. It is exactly as if she has fallen in love with someone who does not love back. She looks up, ahead of this thought. The sun is centered in the sky, a dark hole brightly shrieking. Her heart is its most troubled cry. Each one held/In separate immaculacy.

And what of herself? All that will be left of her is someone recalling she was beautiful at twenty. And perhaps, maybe not even, a slim volume of poems. No use in weighing down people's hands or their hearts. What a terrible thing, she tells herself, to discover it is God in the thoughts and the words that sing in me; God and not Sevi. If I refuse to love back, will He still be able to reach me? I should not want to go to heaven unless I am allowed my own skin, my own separate garden. And yet she also yearns for intimacy and unspent violence.

What of herself? The question persists in her thoughts,

puzzling and baiting her. She distracts herself in the matter of whether fire is the same as heat...

Joyful voices from the hall lead her to think of grass running beneath the roots of trees. She peers into the hall. The flowers at the altar stand like a different kind of forest. How many years of living did it take Don Severino Gil to die? Of dying, to live again? She catches sight of Sevi, wants to run to him but stays. Did one die vein by vein, until the body gave up?

On the second day of the wake, even the three sisters have given up furious crying. They sob when overtaken by proper grief but do not linger in it. Mostly, they are considering what they must do if no will is discovered; how many more chairs and silverware and glasses will be required for the funeral.

Telly smiles to herself. Everyone in the hall looks as if they are merely watching a growing garden. The words they say resemble the names of flowers, resound like many tongues licking.

The voices in the hall swing back and forth, leaving webs on which to catch still other voices. Here is Aurelio Gil saying that the millions being spent on the residence the Pope has spurned could have been spent in regional medical centers, not national institutions to which patients can be brought only with much difficulty from outlying regions. And Maria Esperanza refusing to hear any more of this, nor of the nuclear plant built on earthquake fault lines in Bataan, for which *barrios* have been moved and those remaining have not been informed of what is rising in their midst. "It's blasphemy," she says. "I will not listen."

Telly is comforted by the voices, by the knowledge that Sevi is just behind the wall. There is something sensual in being in a house where everyone has gathered; where by slow or deliberate disengagements sentiments oppose each other but become one finally. She feels held. Grateful, she wills to yield.

A glass of cola is held out to her, a dish of confections. She shakes her head too soon, sending the servant skittering away to others when she wants a taste in her mouth, anything, even what is being offered away from her.

Unsteady voices like old sopranos, full of odd weights and trying to drown other voices, join the corners of the hall, remind her of games of seeking. Full of intrigue in the rising and falling, playing tricks, the voices speak without languages.

She reenters the hall, to act on impulse and surprise herself as well, but stops on seeing Sevi. It terrifies people who live on certainties not to be able to anticipate her. What she wants but will not do is to stand beside Sevi and be spoken to by him, to be picked out from the rest; for him to stay beside her even when others come.

Faded portraits link the dark walls, hang like calendars that have not caught up with the day. Such a strange thing, in the midst of life, someone dies; and in the midst of death, people continuing to breathe. Did she ever pray for her dead mother buried in her wedding clothes? She does not want to be buried. She wants to be turned immediately to ashes, then scattered during a storm. Will Sevi say the cremation rites over her and have heaven – which could be inside a person instead of floating up somewhere – burned and scattered, too? The sky is a false landmark. The sun is on all sides of the house now.

"Telly!" Long thin arms embrace her. "I've been looking for you. All over the city and calling everyone. Why are you so quiet?"

"A headache," Telly gives the excuse relatives expect.

"Can you talk? Good. When I heard Tio Severino died, I thought, Good, I'll go to the wake and find godparents for Clarita's child. The baptism is Sunday. The father is going to Rome, commercial attaché. Too bad not Amsterdam or Tel Aviv, for the diamonds. And Clarita will fly with the older child. Yes. A three-year-old. The baby will be left with me. You'll be godmother, won't you, Telly?"

"Of course. I would haunt you if you did not ask me."

Telly plays along, acts happy. "I thought Clarita was in New York, with that ballet company. Didn't I hear that she got a starring role?" She remembers in time, not the name of her cousin but the circumstances of her life; recalls once envying that nose peaked like a parrot.

"She *was*. Not starring role. They give that to blacks or Chicanos, but Filipinos, never. That's why I do not let my daughters join beauty pageants. I'll die if they are seen parading in a bathing suit. It's all right to wear them for private pools, but be seen on television by even the chauffeurs! And how do I cope with men who will be charging the gates of the house and probably climbing the roof to get a glimpse?"

Telly looks into her purse, just to rest from her cousin's scrutiny. Can she be the one who owns a high-rise hotel?

"You're so lucky, Telly, not to have daughters to worry about. I still have three I have to marry off well. Afterwards, they can get separations or divorces, you know, it's a status symbol to have a Dominican divorce, or whatever. But the baby. It's so pretty, Telly. How can I be a grandmother though? *Lolas* used to wear sayas and kimonas, have their hair tied up in a knot, with gold-trimmed combs and sagging earlobes. That's not me and yet, I'm grandmother. And so are you. You are, too, Telly! This baby is also your *apó*. I can't believe it. We're both *lolas* finally."

"You look like a fairy godmother instead," Telly says, exchanging modesties of a sort, while trying to look for stitches on that stretched and vibrant face.

"Telly, you say the nicest things. I'll remember that the next time somebody calls me a grandmother. I'm so glad you'll come. The child is to be named Farrah. Farrah Stella would be darling. Now, to look for a few more. You haven't seen Finina? I really don't want to ask her, but she has asked me three times to be godmother, so I have to ask her back. But you'll be the principal godmother. The real one. And say, let's go to Geneva together. Have you been to Lucerne? How about Rio?"

116

Yes, Telly agrees, angry with herself for remaining at the wake only because Sevi is there. She has resolved several times to ignore him and here she is thinking of him as if he's an ordinary man who can love back, who can love one person instead of having to include everyone in his heart; here, wondering how his mouth feels, his hands ... She rocks in the warmth of those thoughts, hoping she will remember what she imagines, that it has become the immediate part of endless days. Because she loves him, she feels young, a young girl waiting for someone with whom to fall in love, for whom to be beautiful.

# 4

"It's more than a matter of life and death," Maria Esperanza swears Attorney Sandoval to secrecy, invoking her brother and his death, for if the lawyer is loyal to anyone, it is to Severino. "And not that I need any more property to my name. But . . ." At this point she looks at the casket, yet of course she does not see it clearly. The flowers distract her. The lights flood her eyes. "But the son does not know about such things. Perhaps the property can be put in trust, if it isn't already."

"Perhaps," Attorney Sandoval answers, giving no clue as to whether a will was drawn.

The evasions bait Maria Esperanza's suspicions. She is certain the lawyer is hiding the will. Severino saw him the day before he died just to pass the hour? They discussed something very important, she thinks, and the matter of the Amorsolo painting was just to lead them astray from the truth. And what prevents Sandoval from transferring Severino's property into *his* own name, for nonexistent considerations? Her brother Saturnino did that with their parents' lands and water buffaloes. Everything ended up in his name. She knows of other family fortunes that were lost that way, with the rightful heirs unable to start dissipating them. In any case, she wants Sandoval to speak and trap himself, so she sends nervous messages to Saint Jude and the archangels of battle; and just in case, to Jesus Christ himself, "Lord and Savior, help me now."

In her eighty-three years she has had many occasions of

crucial need and she is used to escalating the terms of bargaining until the favor is granted. She now offers to have candles lighted in all the churches of Manila, including that in Paranaque, in return for saving Father Sevi from completely wasting his inheritance on the poor of his parish.

"He is young," Attorney Sandoval agrees. "He was born after the war, was he not?"

"He is forty-seven! At that age reasonable men have married and begun fortunes to see their family past their death. But what has he done, tell me? A priest's life is so soft. My Jaime is a priest. All he does is say the Mass and teach young men who refuse to act like priests. Jaime worries me. If he has to go to Rome, I have to provide the plane fare. I look after his cassocks. Where do you think he gets his cars? Of course, I do not wish to take back my son from God, or deprive Him of the sons of others. But these priests have to be protected. They know nothing of the world..."

"After the funeral, we can talk about this," Attorney Sandoval remarks, letting the ashes drop between his feet. "I will certainly do my best for you and Severino."

This makes Maria Esperanza more suspicious. Time will give the lawyer opportunity to devise for his own benefit. She looks about for an ashtray, points his attention to it. "Well, I want you to know I am prepared to give Sevi something else in exchange. It's only that the land along the shore is really part of mine, to begin with, and the idea was to give Severino a share, which he never much bothered with in his life. He couldn't be troubled even with things that allowed him to do as he pleased. The farms in Santa Cruz, the *lanzones* plantation he remembered only when he wanted to have a picnic..."

"Land is no longer as safe an investment as before," Attorney Sandoval says. "It is better to have shares in companies that get government contracts. You know how the Ortigas lost their hectares near Meralco. Well..."

"Well, it's still better than having sheets of paper," Maria Esperanza gets cross. Everyone has heard Madame graciously

accepted the offer of a corner by cutting off a large portion of
the land she could see from the roof of the Meralco. Not that
she believes everything she hears. ''And that corner and that
corner and up to that corner and that!'' The mining business.
This is mine and that and this. But what did the Ortigas get in
return? Life spins like a wheel. It's not all loss. Up and down.
Rolling. Administrations and governments come and go.
Good times and bad times.

Attorney Sandoval has lost track of Maria Esperanza's
thoughts. ''We will do something. Don't worry,'' he says,
anxious to leave. The slow arrivals and departures have begun
to make him as uncomfortable as a heavy meal. Besides, the
men did not come until evening and there were mostly
women during the day, and old and older women who do not
excite him.

Maria Esperanza sees her sisters looking towards them,
waiting for an excuse to break into their conversations. They
will have their own ideas but, in the end, what she proposes
will turn out to be the better arrangement. It has always been
like that. She feels her hand being lifted, sees the attorney
standing up to go. ''See if you can find out about the closed
casket. I couldn't sleep all night. Suppose Severino was killed,
was ordered killed? That might not be his body inside.''

''Esperanza!'' Attorney Sandoval scolds. ''If you continue those thoughts you will only disturb yourself and not
only yourself but your sisters as well, and the whole family.
Severino certainly doesn't want that. Specially since he is no
longer here to take care of you.'' His hair is peaked like defiant horns.

Maria Esperanza looks chastened. She wants to be told it is
not so and waits for a firmer denial of her suspicions.

''Peace of mind is worth more than diamonds these days,''
the lawyer relents and bends over Maria Esperanza. ''If it will
help at all, I think Severino has lived an extraordinary life. I
would exchange mine for him, if I could. As for whether his
body is there or not . . . look, a sealed casket seals his memory

in us. We will always think of him young. He never wanted pictures of himself either. Once he began to, and I'm not saying he grew fat, but you yourself know he no longer wanted pictures taken of him. That's it. He planned it this way. To create a mystery perhaps. There's no use in cracking mysteries. They're like mushrooms. Like banana plants. You cut one down and a hundred shoots come up from the roots. That's mystery for you. Severino certainly wants all of us to enjoy peace of mind. And that's the same reason the Pope is coming. For peace. Justice will be done in its own time, if it's not already here. I'll take care of everything. Don't worry. The young son will fulfill his father's wishes and yours, Dona Esperanza.'' He stands erect like a seed bull.

While he talks, Maria Esperanza is chiding herself for confiding in him. She watches him take leave of her sisters, bending over them as he has over her. She wants to call him back, to be the last one assured, but she can barely hold her beads. Although she has taken a nap after breakfast and after lunch, she feels very sleepy. It is barely four in the afternoon. She thinks it is because all she has heard is talk, with Aurelio going on and on about nothing at all, trying to define right and wrong; as if they have all lost their tongues, as if words have dried on their mouths. He is still there talking, talking as if there were resurrection on earth and they would all become young again.

He is looking towards her and she closes her eyes. Clasping the beads in one hand she holds on to the arm of the chair with the other. For the first time that she can remember she wonders if she will wake up the next morning, wonders if she wants to. She opens her eyes as if to see the answer right before her. The light outside is flooding the window, rising on the curtains and drapes like water. The mourners stand about in winding rows like rice seedlings.

# 5

Telly is hurt that Paeng will count her among those she herself dismisses as engrossed in elaborate efforts to appear beautiful. She is particularly hurt because she likes him without reserve. He is a very attractive young man, serious in his bearing and reserved in his manner. Older relatives cannot quite decide what to make of his having been detained at Bicutan. They have not read his student editorials that earned him detention, and they are not particularly interested in hearing him defend Sevi's idea of letting his church stand as it is. "Improving the appearance of the church will give the impression all is well; is just like the government's raising fences around the slums so the tourists cannot see the misery."

No, I would not want him for my son, Telly thinks, and have to worry every night that he might not be coming home for supper. But one like that in a generation is good; interesting, like having different specimen trees in the garden. Telly nods at an uncle who, saying he refuses to listen to anyone younger than himself, starts praising the administration for having model detention camps. "It's not bad," he says. "You should have seen the Japanese camps. We were hung by our thumbnails, made to drink our urine. No, I will not believe that Filipinos can do such things to other Filipinos. The Spaniards did it to us, the Americans; but not Filipinos. I will not believe it even if I see it."

"You have to use your head to get out of these things," a cousin Paeng's age says. "Do you know how I outwitted the

122

commander? I was one of those arrested early in 1973. I pretended I was *baklâ*. Yes, I did. I walked over to him and tried to put my hand on his knee under the desk. Like this and like this and he had no use for me. I talked like this, and made eyes like this and he acted as if ants were crawling underneath his collar. He shouted, 'No more questions for this one. Let him go.' I was just starting to have fun then and I said, 'Sir, I know many things I am willing to tell you . . .' All the time I was moving my shoulders like this and like this.''

Still hurt by Paeng's failure to distinguish her from the others, Telly looks up to Paeng. ''Politics is just one lifestyle, you know. Just one possibility. We can live our lives different ways. We can live in faith, in art. We don't have to waste ourselves on externally exciting things, but we don't have to be raising banners all the time either.'' Her milieu therapist said she should learn to be good to herself so she can be good to others; to get in touch with what she really wants. She asked if it was not against God's will to place herself ahead of the others. ''Is not the way to heaven paved with sacrifice of the self?'' He replied, ''What is your religion?''

Looking up, Telly sees herself and Paeng centered in the mirror across the hall. Instantly she relents and smiles at him. ''You were brave to write the things you wrote . . .''

''Words do not mean anything any more, *Tita*. Government handbills use the same terms, asking us to support democracy by supporting the government. Remember Humpty Dumpty telling Alice scornfully in *Through the Looking Glass*, 'When I use a word it means just what *I* choose it to mean – neither more nor less'? Well, the government has coopted our revolution by calling its dictatorship a 'revolution from the top'. Many are hypnotized, disarmed. The revolt has been defused. How can we rely on mere words?''

''All the king's horses and all the king's men,'' Telly recalls, follows the connections in her mind, ''can't put Humpty Dumpty together again.''

Paeng's mother joins them. "When we finally found where he was being detained, it took weeks you know, all the time I was thinking he was already dead . . . " She is clutching her hands. "It was horrendous . . . we finally found him in Bicutan . . . "

"Where?" Telly is lost in thinking she wants to be beautiful but only for Sevi.

"Bicutan. We got an order for his release on condition that he retract, and this boy who never caused me any trouble, do you know what he says? 'I will not take back a word, Mamá. They can shoot me.' He was prepared to be shot like José Rizal."

Stunned silence gives way to laughter, returns to silence.

Paeng looks embarrassed by the talk of supreme sacrifices, for he does not want to be held with the same regard as the national hero. He merely wanted to emphasize his point.

"You should have let him," an uncle who holds loans guaranteed by the government says. "You young ones should learn how serious it is to bait the authorities. Who is to say the government is wrong? Or that anyone can do a better job than the President? I tell you, there are worse people waiting to take over."

"It's what I felt, Sir," Paeng defends his mother's right to tell her story. "And I still feel it," he adds more softly. "We cannot dismiss the situation so simply as a matter of lesser evil. Our country is all we have. We are all it has. If we do not speak for it, how can it depend upon us?" He turns to tell his mother he is leaving. One man who knows the truth is enough threat to a dictator.

"Go to your grandmother's first. But be back. Your father will come for us. Be careful . . . " She watches him bring the hands of the three sisters to his forehead; sees him, passing Telly again, stop to ask, "Will you come? There is a Mass for detained writers."

The simplicity of Paeng's asking touches Telly. It is as if no explanations are required between them. So she follows him down the stairs without taking leave of anyone. "I read nothing about it," she says, taking his arm part way down the stairs.

He merely smiles. "What newspaper will announce such an event when the official position is that all detainees in political camps have been released? Even the opposition has swallowed that line. Asked to speak, a former senator was surprised. Only when the lists of detained writers were read to him, did he believe. Some have been let go, of course, who are now writing for the government."

"Do you have girl friends?" Telly asks, pulling out her car keys from a large red pocketbook and wondering if his parents gave him enough to indulge himself. "No. Don't answer, I'm an old woman prying." Yet what shall we talk about, she wonders, thinking it inappropriate to ask him about his plans for life. He does not look as if he can take care of himself. Self-fulfilling jobs never paid one's keep and he looks like someone who will be humiliated, destroyed in fact, by having to work for his living.

"I'll drive, Tita." He leads her to his car parked across the street. Instead of answering her question, he asks another of her. "Why are you smiling as if I am a photographer? How can anyone smile these days? When according to the Asian Development Bank we have the highest malnutrition rate in Asia, the lowest per capita daily caloric intake. And the government is responding to this by seeking increased military aid from the United States, Tita. Of course it doesn't mean anything to say that multinationals merely leave behind pollution and an exploited work force, being allowed to expatriate their profits. People who are exploited cannot do anything, those who have privileges . . . " He opens the car door for her. Disco music blares out from the pizza parlor.

"I wasn't, really," Telly protests, sweeping her skirt clear of the door. She waits until he comes over to his side. "I am impressed really. Where do you get those figures? It sounds like the beginning of a modern story, or poem. Not the kind I write but anyway, that."

125

"You did laugh, Tita," he says. So wild is his impatience that he does not look to see if he can swing out of his parking place. "It's all right to worry about the Chileans disappearing in much larger numbers. People can be comfortable comparing figures. They can think themselves safe in this country. I drive fast, Tita. You might want to fasten your seat belt." He swings out into the path of a bus.

"I'm not scared of anything. Least of all of dying," Telly answers. "But if you're going to practise your speech on me, I can be dropped off at . . . "

"All right. No more talk about political and economic domination. Let's see. I really like Father Sevi, my uncle. He's making a stand, too, but not as effectively as he could. He's inhibited by his habit, though there is no reason for it. He knows people can be dehumanized by poverty, but he puts his hopes for a solution on God. At least, that's my impression. I'm sure the cassock does that."

"Other things besides poverty dehumanize." She is thinking of infidelities, as they head down Recto towards Quezon Boulevard. The raised islands of concrete remind her of pantheons. "Other things . . . " Bodies wrapped in ice, waiting to be claimed.

"Of course. His and hers swimming pools. Million peso houses overlooking slums. Excessive wealth and power and privilege. The real subversives are those who grab more than their share and flaunt the inequity."

"You have a one-track mind, Paeng. And not too many girl friends at the moment, I suppose. You say Peace and Justice and Freedom as quickly as I learned to say Jesus/Mary/Joseph." In designer jeans and modified Afros, college girls come out into Recto.

"I'm not too keen about religion. Leo XIII did not intervene for us against the Spanish clergy at the turn of the century. Why should we put our hopes on this Pope's coming? Saints from Japan and China will be canonized ahead of any Filipino, notwithstanding four hundred years of Christianity.

126

Everything is political. And it's not political to give us any recognition. We are a small country, malnourished, exploited by First World countries. So. Let it be. We are a subject people. We ourselves accept this. Who will stand up for us? God won't. The Pope won't..."

"Are you quite finished with your sermon? I was thinking of Baguio today. I love going up and coming down the mountains. The first impact of cold and of heat is as invigorating as a sauna. Would you have come, if I had asked you?"

Tall concrete barriers act like sluices in controlling the flow of traffic towards the Pasig river. Buses, jeepneys and cars rush beneath the overpasses filled with pedestrians holding up umbrellas, pocketbooks and their hands against the sun.

"No. I can't afford the time," Paeng says. They are stalled in front of shops displaying pockets that can convert ordinary pants into designer jeans.

"Of course there's time for Baguio. Too much talk about riding hellbent for one's ideals is just as reckless as all talk about God, in order to think everything will come to the right end. You wouldn't have gone up to Baguio?" She is actually wondering if Sevi would have. There are a lot of places that he could make special by being there with her. But she will not ask him. She is happy enough with her fine yearning.

"There is none," Paeng says, without insisting.

"Suppose..." She cannot think of anything to lure him up there, so she changes her tack. "Just because I ask you. Or Gaddafi offering you 20,000 arms if you go up? Just say yes, even if you do not mean to go. Can't something make you come up?"

He takes the time to throw a look at her. Buildings are blocking out the sky, the roofs of old houses that used to belong to families who financed processions and outfitted inter-island steamers, and called the shots in the past elections.

She creates the sun from its reflections on the shop windows, imagining alleys she has walked through as a child, alleys being lifted up by estuaries and narrow bridges where

127

carts mounted carefully on the thin legs of sleepy horses. She wonders if Sevi ever walked those streets, looked down on the water lilies with purple flowers. Has he ever been led out of the darkness of himself to the light of others? Is that where he is already? What if he never knows he is loved? Is that part of the grace protecting him? She asks herself questions she will not answer. The sidestreets are roads coming out of and into the shadows of old houses.

"I suppose you wished you had not asked me along," Telly says, delighted with her thoughts of Sevi, with being refused by someone she can, by right, command. "You're a stubborn child," she describes herself in Paeng. "But you're right. What we need are memories, not arms. Arms can misfire, be used against the self. But words, writers, memories. Someone should be writing about our times. Silence, self-imposed, serves the censors. Just a diary, of what martial law has forced one person to become..." She leans away from the seat. The cloth is stuck to her back with sweat. It feels like a hand. Poems are a kind of diary, too. But some people think poems are nothing. Poems are all I want to do. The church, before whose front door bombs once burst into the opposition rally, comes up on Telly's right. She knows without looking to the side. All I want to do are poems. I want to die, too, Telly thinks. Are they the same thing? Black clouds come out of the exhaust of converted jeepneys. Suppose God is just a type of virus that takes over one's body, becomes one's body.

"A country without memories," Paeng is saying, picking up Telly's thoughts. He tries to recall something in his past, from the day before, but cannot. He cannot recall seeing Telly before.

"I remember when I first saw you," Telly places the red pocketbook between them. "You were climbing a *duhat* tree, shaking the branches and making the dark fruit drop and roll. Some fell on my white dress, staining it." She looks up through the electric wires criss-crossing the boulevard, making an unruly forest of the sky. "Do you remember that? I was angry, said you were spoiled. You must still be spoiled. Imagine telling your mother you preferred to be shot in Bagumbayan. You could have stopped her heart!''

''Do you, too, faint when you want to, like my mother?''

She refuses to be just a variation of anyone. ''I recall, part of the same afternoon, red flowers, the kind one pulls apart to disclose the nectar which one sucks. Tiny flowers, stuck with thorns; and fitting cross-legged with red fingernails, on the *azotea*.'' She recalls the house in Santa Ana, recalls herself young in it. ''You and your parents were visiting that afternoon. An uncle, grandfather to you, Lolo Piring, was there, too. He was wearing the white starched suit popular in the early part of the century. A white handkerchief was in his breastpocket, as wilted as a withered flower; a Panama with a white band...How clearly I see it!''

''What does it mean?'' Paeng feels his conscience being tempted.

''Nothing. Only that we live in each other's memories.'' Telly sits forward, hands on her knees as if she is back on that porch, rocking. ''When I am gone, who will remember Lolo Piring in his white starched suit, sitting in the garden? It is as if all his life was being lived so that he could sit in the garden that afternoon and so I could see him and, years and years later, recall him to someone who was there as a boy and does not remember that particular afternoon. You see, I'm passing on to you my memory of him...'' On the verge of tears, she looks away between the buildings towards the Bay. She thinks of the palms which she cannot see but that she knows are there, within the reach of the sea sprays, the fronds glistening. Often, in the hospital outside New York City she was crying and remembering at the same time as if those two things were one. ''Don't look, Paeng. I'm an old woman crying. Don't look at me. I don't want you to remember me crying.'' She wipes her face with her fingers. She tries to think of something else, of the pagoda and the mosque that came into view before they mounted the bridge that used to be the Colgante, the swinging bridge.

Paeng keeps his question to himself. Why do people cry when their lives appear to have no reason for it? Is it the same as old houses, the ones they passed in Quiapo, which have become rooming houses? They look to him like a ruined forest, not because he remembers them when they were grand, but because of the laundry hanging at the windows, the cracked *capiz*-shell panes.

As a child, crossing the Colgante after having ice cream at the Magnolia kiosk, which is now the Department of Education housed in quonset huts left over from the US Army barracks, she used to be frightened she would slip between the wooden trestles and land on the waterlilies, so she would drop lemon candles which she hoarded in her pockets, some kind of offering in place of herself. In the orphanage on the island an old priest who could have become archbishop and cardinal died in a cell along the corridors reserved for old unwanted people. She imagines him stretched in death, powerfully asleep.

Having stopped speaking, they keep their thoughts to themselves. Piecing together what Telly has said into a movable puzzle, Paeng thinks she is right. The essence of tyranny is not the leaders so much as the people who absorb it into their lives, multiply it until it becomes not just part of a country's unhappy heritage but its unholy tradition. He is surprised that she leads him to this conclusion, she who is so well dressed that she might just have come from a modeling session at the Manila Hotel or Hyatt. The essence of tyranny ... If he says something about this at the meeting after the Mass, will she even recognize her thoughts in his? He looks at her without turning, sees the flush that deepens her cheek and darkens her eye, making her as fragile as a fading portrait; a miniature on ivory, glass on which itinerant painters used to paint madonnas. We live in each other's memories, he will say; or not at all. We are each other's opportunities, each other's promise.

How could he have felt, inside the house on Recto, that she

was one of those painted on air, a mere impulse that passed without registering; full of frivolous details? No one has ever surprised him as much as she has; and he is grateful.

All the shadows, to Telly, have become as large as mountains. Her thoughts are running strangely ahead of the traffic past the buildings of the early American Occupation. She recalls the shadows winding luxuriously on the bannisters, and looks towards the Bay, thinking of the incredibly beautiful sunsets she and Quiel watched from the Luneta Hotel the first days of their marriage and the strange feeling that came upon her that she had done something against herself by marrying him. Did she know even then that he would not be faithful? Is it madness then to run through flames, away?

Paeng thinks again of what crossed his mind as they entered Liwasang Bonifacio, heading towards Taft. Having caught sight of her looking at him, her mouth childlike, now he understands what Father Sevi had said during the Mass: ''We're part of the splendor of the Father...'' It is a pain; and a burden; and a joy. As if she hears his thoughts, she looks at him; imagining wells rising to the top.

The sunlight reflected on the oncoming cars on Taft makes fine lines that shatter her face. My God, he thinks, she's old enough to die. The lines tear her face apart like claws. But then he thinks back to a poem that vaguely went: As soon as one is born, one is old enough to die. At that moment, as if a bell has rung, he would gladly have given up his life to add his unused years to hers.

She looks away again. Designer clothes in the couturier shops distract her. Sequins are now out. Oversize sleeves, flared skirts and glass slippers are out... A scent comes to her, making her think that she has not seen a *camia* in a long, long time. Did they no longer bloom? It feels as if she has never seen those pale petals bloom from bud.

Afraid she will see his thoughts on his face and laugh at the flimsy offering of himself, pitiful before what other men must have offered her, Paeng fastens his eyes on the jeepneys cutting

131

into his lane. The sounds of traffic have the sound of struggle: currents opposed in the river.

A child being carried astride a hip brings Telly's thoughts back to Sevi through herself. She is angry that he will not even know how she feels. As if Paeng is about to press his brakes, she puts a hand out to the dashboard, then immediately clutches herself by the arms as if they have hit the child she hit in Tondo earlier that day. How terrible memory is. It brings guilt and pain; without being able to invent joy.

Glaring at the traffic lights that change suddenly, Paeng tells himself that it is not fair. All his life, from then on he will be looking for someone like her. She doesn't even know the pain she is causing; would not care if she knew, would only laugh, be amused, toss it away like another compliment. Such things must no longer astonish her heart. So he wishes he had not come to the wake, had not been introduced to her, had not asked her to come along. But then, it is none of her doing, this painful longing he can neither explain, nor wish away, nor properly endure; that runs along his body like fingertips.

So he whistles. The sound jams in his throat. He tries to bring himself to reason by telling himself she expects men to behave this sacrificial involuntary way in her presence. It is what nourishes her and women like her. Unless they are lavishly admired, they wither.

As this thought crosses his mind, she turns to smile at him. "I can taste sugar ants," she says, "and I have not eaten any sweets." Like roots that have run out of earth, electric wires hang overhead. If it is meant to confound him, he determines it will not work. She will not have her way with him. He will wish her away as he told his father he would wish away temptations. He was thirteen then, being initiated in what is expected of men and resenting the inevitability. In the course of his explanations, his father said, "Paeng, we men have to love someone we cannot have. It makes us work harder to prove ourselves. Each man needs someone to whom he will give his life and who disdains it, who ignores it or who is unaware of it." He wonders if his father ever loved Telly; and if his mother knew. Or is it merely a romantic thought shared, in order to prepare him for the time when he is not loved back? He tries to whistle once more and chokes on his spit.

"Someone is thinking of you," Telly says. "Is she young and beautiful? Wrong question; too many words. Is she beautiful? You're blushing. It means you're sensitive. Your blood is close to the surface, leaps instead of sleeping in your flesh. You'll make someone very happy someday, Paeng. But don't wish it to be forever. A moment is enough. Don't answer. You don't have to say anything. I'm an old woman speaking. Ignore my prying . . . Suppose we're late?"

At that moment he cannot think of the name of anyone, cannot remember any face although he has, before this, felt the urgency of being in love, the extravagance of desiring, burning and powerful, because in danger of being denied its fierce insistence.

Is it someone like Clarita whose child's godmother she will be? Telly recalls a young girl who, planning to be a premiere danseuse of an international ballet corps, swam sixteen laps in the morning before the sun came up over the hedge of hibiscus, thereafter drinking a cup of vinegar to keep her flesh from disfiguring her bones. Did she know even then that something would happen to disfigure her dream?

"I hope no one dies for a long time," she says aloud, "even if it means we shall not be seeing each other again. Why should relatives gather only for wakes?" her body is stretching inside her white dress. She feels young and lean but not beautiful. She remembers most clearly that she never felt beautiful. Always someone else was taller and finer. Her body is not what she wants. It prevents her from loving herself. People are either polite or sarcastic, she thinks, when they pay her compliments. Their attention only makes her feel uglier. There have been weeks when all she did was sleep; when she walked about her darkened house, all windows shut, refusing to notice the mirrors. Once, it was not a dream, she looked into a mirror and saw nothing. For a long moment, she saw nothing. But I no longer want to be beautiful. She can think of herself dreaming of cousins' children, all the children she will never have. She thinks she might be a religious at heart, a dilettante in outlook, a profligate in attire. I am what I am not. Should she want to be beautiful only for him?

Long after she sees it, she wonders if the look she caught on Paeng's face is one of hurt. It's not, definitely not, the look of a dumb or intoxicated man. Yet how is it possible when he is so self-possessed, so certain he is going to turn the country about and send it running back to its ideals? He gives her the impression that he is looking down from a height even while he also looks up from himself, which is good.

"You should write about us, Paeng," she says, "a long novel, say: *The Gils of Manila*. You might tape the older relatives who remember the revolution against Spain and the War against the Americans; those who fought against the Japanese. They live for a while in us; then after we go . . . Is that too sentimental? You're a writer. Invent prophecies for us."

"No, Tita. I'm not the one to do it. I can't sit at a desk while the country plunges to its doom, ransacked by men who claim to be saving it." Her question allows him to close his heart again, after it surprised him by opening with such a fierce longing to be loved back right then, right there but also forever.

"Call it *Unassembled Lives*," Telly says, turning her full attention upon him, daring him to take his eyes off the traffic and look at her, too. "Or: *Unattempted Lives*."

He withdraws the hand he never placed on her. He is nothing to her, and to himself, to the earth. Nothing. He will only discover for himself that nothing can be changed even while change goes on. He must be grateful for unexpected moments. He is grateful that she will try to make him create. He knows that it is one way of refusing to become either a mere consumer or a product, but right now there are more important things than what he will make of himself.

"Writing is another way of loving God," Telly says. "It is another gift to him. Don't you think so?"

His thoughts cannot bridge the gap she has crossed in hers, and he thinks he mishears her.

"It's a fine gift of ourselves." She is thinking quite oddly of those children who will have no experience of any government but that of martial law. What kind of ideals will they have when they will not know how it is to be free, when what they will have perfected is the art of being left alone, of thinking what is safe to say? "Sometimes we have to be pushed before we will fight for our lives. And writing is fighting for our lives."

He is concentrating on cutting into the right lane in order to turn onto Herran.

"Call your characters types disguised as real people, then you will offend no relative anxious to be offended. Say they are wholly their own responsibility, being the figment of their imagination," Telly says, thinking of a proper disclaimer for his novel.

He is thinking, as he turns, of what he might say if he is called upon to speak. Something about refusing to be a token rebel. "Purveyor of token dissent." About being one of those not interested in the rewards of the government and its New Society, and therefore not apt to be tempted into joining it. "This is not the society Rizal set out to establish. It's a far lesser and more dangerous dream. The real measure of ourselves is not the ideals of the New Society, but lies outside it. When the administrators of Martial Law take part in the so-called protest plays, when they pose as the revolutionaries and the successors of Luna and Mabini, it is not only our history that is destroyed but time as well. We cannot be our ancestors and our descendants. Bullshit! And a righteous and grand dictator is a dictator nevertheless. We should not be lulled into equating the absolute authority required in households and *haciendas*, for the sake of harmony, with the obedience required for the sake of peace and order in the country. Nowhere is it proper..."

He remembers Telly, looks at her quickly as he hunts for a place to park. She must feel like a fugitive, too. It is also possible his mother has asked her to talk sense into him, to protect him from his young feelings. The happiest men are those who never seek the sun for never having seen it, who let the rain come when it will and stand meekly waiting, like trees, to receive it.

He wants to make it rain, while the sun is shining.

# 6

Inside St. Paul's auditorium, Telly has a feeling of something coming nearer and nearer, but unseen; so she sits far off to one corner to watch the last-minute preparations for the Mass. Paeng, of course, is soon in the midst of the group, now with those strumming impromptu compositions on their guitars, or with those pacing themselves in the reading of verses written by rebels from Balagtas through Rizal, and on to those still detained, whose poems have somehow been smuggled out. One young man is wearing a shirt on which has been printed, inside a detention camp, secretly: Free Political Prisoners in the Philippines.

She feels envy watching them. If she had had a cause as serious as these bright young ones, she might have gotten over her hurt, in time to do something with her life. She wonders what her doctor in Katonah would say to this. He made no assumptions, not even how God might judge his actions or his thoughts. Telly cannot imagine how this is possible. She would feel herself adrift unless anchored in the certainty of someone thinking of her; if it has to be, even God. Even if that certainty has to be in constant flux, matching moments of belief and unbelief.

Someone sits down beside her. "Hi." She replies to the greeting; but because she never believes people remember who she is, she does not feel compelled to say more. On the other hand, she remembers everyone she has met, not their names always, but their faces certainly and what they have said. To some of them she responds in her thoughts, in her poems.

She smiles, thinking of the small cafe across from the college where Paeng took her for ice cream that was astonishingly rich in its *ubi* flavor. She had *barquillos* from Iloilo with it and enjoyed watching young college students standing in line at the copying machine. Then the lights dimmed. Power failure. The look on Paeng's face as they came out into the street suggested that he was thinking of sabotage. But once in the assembly hall of St. Paul's, Paeng brightened up, took matters in hand with the Prison and People Apostolate of the Church.

When she was not yet deeply in herself, when she was as young as the *colegialas* in their black and white plaid skirts and white blouses . . . She lost her thought in the freshness of the faces. How sad, she thinks, that faces disappear. Perhaps years and generations later faces reappear, features suddenly return; but by then no one is there to recall the faces from which they have come. She will never have any odd or sweet variation of herself; nor Quiel from her, nor Sevi.

"Are you a poet?" A young man sits beside her.

"Not really. Are you?"

"Sometimes. I'm reading one of my poems. I wrote it in detention and I'm afraid it might be too strong. I wrote it not to be read aloud. I wish someone else would read it. Would you?"

She smiles, shaking her head. And the young man leaves to walk over to the *colegialas* setting up the gifts to be brought to the altar.

The directress of the club sponsoring the Mass announces that a message has come from someone who cannot attend. From the back someone answers: "Only death and detention serve as the excuse for not being present. Let's not read the paper of anyone who does not come." The tone is playful but it rests on anger.

Paeng walks over to explain to Telly. "We'll start as soon as the priest arrives. You're not bored yet, are you?"

She shakes her head. Full of regrets, she wishes she had not come. Her doctor used to say she dwelled in the past, trying to reassemble it into the continuous present. "Do you ever look ahead?" She does not look forward to anything.

Telly recognizes a leading writer, winner of prestigious awards, to whom she has been introduced at every place they have met. Unexpectedly, he says to her, "I'm trying to decide if I absolutely must receive communion."

"Is that crucial?" Telly asks. Does everything have to be political, as Paeng believes?

"If I do, it will be the third time in my life. The first was my First Communion. The second, when I was married. I could not get away from either one."

A sheet of paper is being passed to them. "It's the most important document to come out of this Mass," the young man passing it says. He offers a pen, which Telly does not take. She has her own Staedtler 01, its point like a hypodermic needle. While she signs, the young man says, "This is a testimonial not to the detained writers – they have done their part; but to those who have the courage to come here in person. Thanks."

Telly feels a hand on her shoulder. She does not expect to see Jaime and she looks at him without any expression.

"It's me," Jaime says. "When I left the house, Mamá was wondering where you were. She can't abide disappearing acts, you know. You have to sign her log book."

"You're saying Mass?" Telly cannot believe anyone will choose him when she has never seen him do anything devoutly. When it was announced that he was to be ordained, some relatives said, "He might as well since he cannot, like his father, remain faithful to any woman."

"I delayed a trip to Lausanne for this. Luckily I did, or I would have missed Uncle Severino's wake, he and I were going to Athens once. I can't recall why we never took the trip."

"Is that for a religious congress, or whatever you call those things?" Telly tries to sound as sarcastic as she can.

"No. My annual high retreat for rejuvenation. It's the only

time I can be by myself without Mamá or the Father Rector looking over my shoulder. I go to museums, to plays. I go by motorcycle. I hike. And I meet all kinds of people. Then I can come back to burn my life at the altar!''

''I didn't see much burning from you yesterday.'' Telly refuses to be disarmed. ''You know, I still can't believe you're a priest. Probably nothing will convince me you're not really impersonating someone else. Are you waiting for Tia Esperanza to die so you can turn into the real you?''

''Telly, you're a nuisance but nice. Come off it. What do you want me to bring to you from Europe? I'm bringing everyone something, I might as well add another package. Just nothing over five pounds or taller than I am. I'm serious. What have you set your heart on?''

''Nothing,'' she answers but immediately reconsiders. ''Yes, I want something. Everyone wants me to get married again. So, bring me someone taller than you are by just a bit, not so heavy, not too bright since I need a lot of silence, and not too rich so he won't have the heart of a playboy, not too saintly since I need a bit of fun occasionally. And you don't have to have it wrapped. You can lead it down the runway. I'll be there to take it away from you.''

''It's done.'' He places his arm about her. ''You just might be surprised. Now, I think that's the signal to start thinking religion. Stay awhile, Telly. Let's have dinner afterwards. There's a marvelous new French restaurant. Mussels with garlic and real quiche. Fluffy and not as thick as a pie.'' He lets her go, then pulls her by the arm. ''Listen, why not go to Lausanne? We can keep an eye on each other and Mamá will not have to worry. You send her reports about me and I'll do the same for you. Notarized and signed. With imprimatur.'' He winks at her and is gone.

He reappears solemnly robed for the entrance antiphon. The choir sings ''We Are the Light of the World'' as the entrance hymn. Their voices break against several empty chairs...

Paeng and the illustrious writer are to bring gifts to the altar. She lets herself be filled with the singing until it is inside her. It is with some surprise that she hears Jaime saying, "We are God's own work and He likes what He created. In us, through whom God is present in the world, Jesus is incarnated. So when we remember our deaths, our lives and our dreams, we remember Jesus' life, His death, and His hope for us. When we write our poems, we take part in the creation of His world on earth. Artists who are true to their vision are the saints of the earth. Their communion is with those in heaven. When we take part honorably in government, when we produce the crops, when we serve each other, as well as when we say Mass, we put together our strengths and our love so that his work on earth can be accomplished..."

Telly cannot look at Jaime, afraid he will see the surprise in her eyes. She catches Paeng looking at her and hides her eyes in the skirt draped over her knees.

"... Let us ask of each other then: Why is it that we know what it takes to be a patriot, but do not become one; know what holiness means, yet make no effort to be closer to God? We all know what justice demands; and yet do nothing to create or to restore it. We recognize truth; but we allow those who declare it to be denounced; allow them to languish in prison, to succumb to torture. Why is it that it is very unpopular to do what we know is right? Only a handful of us are here when the hall could have been filled, could have overflowed. Why? As if we are not in this world to prepare for the next, as if God's kingdom is not only secret but imagined, no more real than a dream, an illusion...."

Here, Telly thinks, unwilling to say it even to herself, is every part together of Father Jaime Gil, man of conscience. Her admission is painful, like lifting herself over a wall imbedded with broken glass. How dreadfully she feels her earlier simple dismissal of Jaime. It burned itself out like a fire, Telly tells herself, trying to disown her earlier judgment. Is there a way, without speaking, of asking to be forgiven?

The particular sequence and combination of the day's happenings – the child falling under her car, the cafe that suddenly darkened, the tree in the *azotea* and the drying flowers – come over her again like strong waves that rearrange the shore, and she has to go and be by herself, in case she cries. She finds her way out into the courtyard. By the time she reaches the street, she knows she wants to die. Right there and then. Again.

It is strange, she thinks, that this wish should follow so closely her discovery that Jaime is very probably a good man, though he does not appear devout. She walks along Herran heading for Taft, knowing that the rest of the message of the Mass is something she has lost forever.

Her problem comes to her soon enough. God has to be special in men's lives, but man cannot be special in his. And she wants to be special even when she claims humility. This thought makes her pull down a hand she has raised to flag a taxi. Why can't I go by common jeepney? she asks herself. She waves at one. The driver does not see her hand in time to stop at her corner. He slows down, waits for her beyond the stand of people hoping to catch their ride home, but seeing a traffic cop approach, speeds away. She has run in vain for a ride, in full view of many people. She holds her head disdainfully but inside she is crushed. Souls must have their own scent, Telly thinks. Mine must smell sticky, like fish. She is forced to wait for a ride, in her white shoes.

Confused, she cannot even imagine that, back in the auditorium of St. Paul's, the list of detained writers is being read instead of the Common prayers; that Jaime is saying, "We lose our freedom to our leaders if they do not act with justice, if they arrogate to themselves powers to which they have neither the right nor the authority. We have lost our independence to our leaders. And what can we do?"

Paeng turns around, sees Telly gone from the community declaring themselves against oppression.

"Each one of us must decide," Jaime continues, "to whom

he will be faithful. To God, or to the government which is not faithful to the people. First, we must know to whom God is faithful: to us whom He created, or to the State which we created. By doing this, we choose before whom to tremble.''

Paeng shifts in his seat. These are the words he wishes he himself had written.

''I will tell you what one man did. His relatives thought he lived only for himself, because that was what he was doing most of his life. But during the last months, unknown to these relatives and to his friends, he was going to the detention centers in order to list the names of those incarcerated without charges. In this way, they could no longer disappear without trace. He informed their relatives where they were, helped pay for the defense of those without means. I can't tell you how he got such a calling. I was surprised to meet him in one such camp. Well, that man is now dead. A wake is even now being held for him. I would like to suggest that when we offer our prayers for the writers who are in detention, who have died in detention, that we include this man in our pleas.'' He looks up and does not see Telly.

''I will not tell you his name. It will not mean anything to you. Besides, he did not wish to be singled out and praised, though he should be. He was expiating sins, mostly his own; not to prove he was good and praiseworthy, but to express his desire to be good, to be at peace. Peace is a gift from God; given, not deserved. Upon it all relationships rest ... For this reason, this man wanted to remain unknown. But God knows he is in our intentions, the same way that the faith of the dead is known to Him alone ... ''

It is not for us to judge, Jaime Gil thinks as he pronounces the blessing. He is not surprised that Telly has left. He cannot imagine anyone being able to live with her, cannot imagine her being able to live with herself. Still, he wishes her peace.

She is, Father Jaime always thought, capable of asking for

143

John the Baptist's head on a platter; and also, without her knowing it, of entertaining the angels. She has been made only a little lower than they.

# 7

Telly is still troubled. Her fear is that God will no longer leave her alone, so she tells herself not to trust Jaime completely, on the principle that no one can really be trusted. Certainly not the sun/Suppose it stopped shining/After one learns to expect it?/And flowers are too/Raucous/They root in the cracks of thoughts/Thinking to make one yield/Stones are safer/But even with stones/One risks remembering/And promising/And air adorns itself/With fragrance/Cunning enough/To break into sealed/Flesh...

Confused that a man who, from the time they were children, was so openly pleased with himself, can also be sensitive and in such a moving way, Telly refines her guilt. I should have stayed, she thinks: I come like the bearer of negative gifts/Unable to put my intensity/To other purpose/Than myself. In the darkness of the avenue she pleads: I'm afraid.

Her doctor told her, ''You're insecure. We all deserve to be, unless we're fools or saints. But take a bold baby-step forward and see what happens. You have everything going for you, yet you refuse to believe it. I think you're afraid to be loved because you might not be able to love back, might not deserve being loved. So you run from man to man. You seek one who cannot love you, so you'll feel safe...Believe in yourself.''

Not knowing how to get home by jeep or by bus, Telly walks along Taft, waiting for someone to come and take her where she wants to go. Impulsively, she boards a jeep after some girls who have managed to flag it down. Inside, she leans back. Her body simply droops. Next to her a man is smoking furiously, careless of where the ashes fall. She looks down at her fingers and is startled to see her rings. Unless one travels in a car, it is dangerous to wear jewels in Manila. Even inside cars stopped at intersections, earrings can be snatched along with necklaces. She twists the gems around to her palms. But I'm really afraid not of losing my rings, but of being deprived of what I own, of being assaulted. Even if nothing is taken, knowing a thief has entered one's rooms makes one feel violated.

None of the passengers seem to have noticed her jewels. Perhaps, they assume them to be fake or she would not be wearing them so openly. This thought makes her angry. She twists her rings around, baring their sparkle. Nothing happens.

The jeep passes the Jai Alai, where she once danced in the skylit terrace; the Columbian Club which is moving to Santa Ana. She closes her eyes, refusing to see landmarks. As a little girl she used to close her eyes when *calesas* started mounting the steep bridges over the estuaries. The horses' struggle to carry the carriage over the crest, to keep from rolling back in the effort to ascend, returns to her as the jeep runs up the bridge towards Quiapo. What she sees when she opens her eyes is the large church around which is a fence of baskets on which candles have been lighted. She follows the girls out of the jeep, failing to pay her fare.

She crosses on the overpass from where she watches the jeep heading for Espana. She will have to leave the money in the church. How much, she does not know. She walks past the carriages which carry the Nazarene in processions, aware of darkness lying inside the glass in the shape of human figures. She does not turn to look but walks into a pew, kneels and waits for words to come to her, waits to feel some words in her head the way she felt beads through her fingers. Words with which to postpone wanting to die, and death. Poems postpone suicide, her doctor said.

Was she born with a seed to self-destruct? She knows one can go through the motions of life without reasons for being alive. Wearing jewels, it is possible to adore darkness and mortality. Are her poems incantations to the child inside her that wants to die? That has to die? Or are they her vocation, the means by which she stays alive, moment by moment staving off mortality?

She is startled to see a man offering perfumed cotton to her. She hesitates, then accepts. He waits, expecting her to do something more besides accepting. Disappointed, he moves on to other women down the aisle, who reach into their pocketbooks for something to place on the man's other hand.

While the lights of candles bend around the tall shadows in the church, Telly holds the soft wad in one hand. She does not know it has been used to clean the Black Nazarene that afternoon but, suspecting it to be an object of worship, she clutches it in her hand. The statue of Saint Anthony catches her attention as she gets up. Genuflecting, she looks up at the *sampaguita* necklaces hanging from its toe.

Leaving by another door, she finds herself at one corner of Plaza Miranda, facing Carriedo and Evangelista. The smell of herbs useful in aborting foetuses, in relieving cramps, neuralgia, every conceivable pain and spasm draws Telly towards the darker and narrower street whose end is not visible from the Plaza. She feels like a stranger, for she does not know how to act in those premises. Attempting to find her way out of the tangle of lights and wares she runs into a woman who holds up a deck of cards to her: ''Have your fortune told!''

Telly does not intend to deal with the woman, who follows her. When a parked jeep forces Telly to turn around, the woman sets up a stool for her on the sidewalk, against hanging cloths. ''Pay only half price, ten pesos. I'm on my way home. I just need ten pesos to buy cough medicine for my child. I won't take long, missis.''

The lights and shadows, the flowing colors of the cloths incant Telly with invisible words and she sits down behind the parked jeep.

"Tell me. What is it you want, Miss?" The woman shuffles the cards. Her fingers are immaculately polished. As sharp as claws, her nails stab the air. Intently, Telly watches the woman's hands. She is asked to cut the deck twice. The colors of the square board covered with purple wrapping paper distract Telly. She sits still, waiting for something to be conjured within the corners.

"It might not happen right away," the woman says, laying out the cards in deliberate patterns, "but you will own a house..."

"I already have a house." She digs her stiletto heels into the pavement, just inches away from the edge along which flows water that could have been bottled for mystifying ailments.

"A car?" the woman turns another card over, obviously not expecting Telly to have this, too. Seeing her about to nod, the woman quickly opens up another card, and another, "A trip abroad, to America and to Europe, jewels..."

Telly is intrigued. "Tell me something I want," she encourages the woman to devise if she has to, to find the ends of her thoughts.

"*Hatiin pô ninyo, uli.*" The woman looks at Telly with more respect than before. "You have everything my clients pray for. Let's see if the cards have more for you than you have. *Hatiin pong muli* – cut the deck again, please."

Telly cuts the cards. She is holding her breath. She can smell candles and flowers and a sweet wind blowing from the sea, mixed with the smell of clothes salvaged from fires and spread out on the sidewalk in the other street. The odd blending enthralls her. She tries to anticipate the cards. "Tell me. What do they say?" She is willing the cards to speak for her, to say she will have the man she has waited for in dreams and baited with unsaid words.

"The cards are good. Look at this and this. See. here is what you want and will have!" The woman exults.

"Where?" Telly trips over the sharp fingernails that stab

148

the board and scratch the purple black. She is smiling, her hands halfway to her face. Her heart is lifting, rising from interminable dreams towards its morning.

"Here. The cards say it. You will have a son. A healthy boy!" The woman speaks proudly, as if presenting her with the body.

Telly's eyes fall away from the cards, from the board and from the woman's fingernails. She stands up, flinging a ten peso bill onto the board, and walks away from the draped cloths and the parked jeep and the woman's anxious cry, "What is it you want? Tell me."

Watching Telly walking away down Evangelista, the woman gathers her cards and the board. Other fortunetellers look curiously as she passes them on the way back to Plaza Miranda. She shrugs her shoulders at them. "All kinds of people," she says, "that's what's in the world these days. It doesn't surprise me. She's crazy."

Then having explained herself, the woman stops to buy a few strands of *sampaguita*-garlands, carefully selecting those with flowers still budded white. Next, she buys a red candle shaped like an angel. Only then does she enter the church and, kneeling her way towards the altar, brings her gifts forward.

Along the aisles are other offerings, spreading their secret scents and wax upon the figured tiles worn by thousands of knees beseeching God for favors of health and enough to tide them over the present need. She sets up her candle, pulls out her rosary of white plastic beads. Praying for her own dreams, she suddenly thinks of Telly. What can she want? the fortune-teller wonders. What can any woman possibly want?

# 8

It is the second and last night of the wake for Don Severino Gil, and already the three sisters feel as if they have been in his house all the days of their lives because they have been re-membering all their dead and thinking of themselves dying. They struggle against their thoughts, which still keep coming unannounced and uninvited, like coarse answers from dark futures.

They sit in their chairs, as far from the casket and the altar as they have ever been, waiting for people to come and lift their grief. Those who have come before, a second, a third time, have lost interest in talking and replaying all the exhausting sequences of their lives. They sit around silently as if, should they speak, they would only unsay what they have spoken.

Now and then someone, with much effort, gets up to tell the scattered clusters a moment recalled. "Did you see Sever-ino when he was eighteen and was Constantino at Tia Inez' *Santa Cruz de Mayo?*" And the others who are old enough to share those memories, look into themselves, fall silent until they can see once more the shimmer of lights, hear the clear and vibrant singing: *Dios te salve, Maria; Llena eres de Gracia*; feel again the fragrant silkiness of their young skin. For them, time is the criminal, no matter how far away in memories as rich as dreams they are able to get – in their present bodies, flesh gets in the way of their comfort; – and guilt is time's accomplice for so many acts done wrong, left undone and for-feited. Now they fear hell almost with the fear of children whose faces have been rubbed against holy pictures showing Satan pulling a dying man into eternal fire, his tail curled like a shark's, his eyes balls of flame. Their thoughts provoke the wish that if earth is hell, then they can escape it with their death.

The young ones who drift in and out are amused by the words that only partly restore those memories. They cannot understand the preoccupation with death and afterlife. If they recall their lessons about Paradise at all, they place it in Africa, before the continent, in their imagination, turned into a dark desert. So they watch the old ones, stringing them against the walls where their old-fashioned carved chairs stand, as if they are beads of a necklace badly designed. Yet something makes them stay awhile, whether it is pity or a vague, disturbing feeling that they are looking at themselves in the future. Quickly enough the feeling gives way to the certainty of what they want from life: trips abroad for which they will work as stewardesses and ticket checkers if parents or grandparents cannot be coaxed into sending them there, sportscars, Pentax cameras and all the enticing merchandise that dominate their young dreams and turn their whims into absolute needs.

And those in between, who still have years of fun, of making things happen, of risking themselves to prove they are fully in control of their lives, they cannot be frightened by truth for they, somehow, trust in lies to overcome every threat; not outright lies or evil lies, but lies that make truth bearable, a mere discomfort that passes. If they speak at all of the matter, they say they do not expect to live into old age, do not want to; and they pass on to the young ones the advice that had been given them: Don't do anything you will live to regret; adding their own discovery that life is too short. "It's here, it's gone."

The men look off into space, out of the window, up at the ceiling that is high enough for them to think of the sky opening and angels in bikinis descending.

151

"Have we had supper?" Maria Esperanza looks toward the dining table. It is still set. Every newcomer is pressed to partake of the meal, is tempted with stuffed chicken *galantina* and soups and a variety of stews cooked the way they have been cooked in each household, and pastries and fruits and *dulces*. Someone always asks for something out of season as if the seasons have merged because Don Severino Gil is dead.

"There is still a whole *relleno*," Maria Paz declares, unwilling to hazard an answer, suddenly not knowing herself if they have had supper.

"There are three more in the refrigerator," Maria Esperanza corrects her. "I had them stuffed this morning. They can be saved for tomorrow."

"There's a lot of ice cream," Maria Caridad says. She has a sweet tooth. If she could have her way, she would eat only pastries and ice cream. Her pockets are jammed with candies and chocolates which she craves and which her children airmail from America. She brings pieces of cake to bed, and in the morning ants have nested under her pillow.

"It's so hot," Maria Esperanza says, looking at the window as if guests might be entering that way, too. "It's so hot."

But electric fans are whirring in every corner. The one overhead is throwing the shadows of its dark arms on the altar and the flowers, passing over the guests like wings.

Standing or sitting, the men stare in separate directions as if waiting for different revolutions to call them to arms.

"It's really hot," Maria Paz agrees, fanning herself with a Mass card from the pile that has been given the family. Her thumb is fat on the white cross on the cover. Her sweat beads the arms of the cross, making it look dark and broken.

"It will be hotter still tomorrow," Maria Caridad says, not looking forward to walking in the funeral. She expects to faint. She has fainted at every funeral. No, she cannot recall ever watching a casket being lowered into the ground, and she cannot therefore brace herself properly for the next morning. She

152

glances at her brother's casket, recalling having heard of people who had died fighting for breath inside, of men digging up caskets so the bones can be reinterred inside a church and finding the inside of the coffin badly scratched...

"I hope it cools down when the Pope is here. Can you imagine him in his robes in this kind of heat?" Maria Esperanza worries.

"It's too bad Severino will not see him," Maria Caridad cries softly. The tears fall evenly down her cheeks.

"I'm so tired," Maria Esperanza says. "I could sleep now, but I won't."

"I could sleep, too," Maria Paz says. "But it's the last night and I will keep awake. Dom wants to give me something to make me fall asleep." She mentions her son who is a doctor, who specializes in cancer and has no time to visit her because he has more patients than he wants. "Foreigners travel across the world to come to him," she adds. "Even his professor at Harvard came to consult him." She pulls herself up, places an arm on the sides of her chair, sitting up so still and precisely, obsessed with holding exact positions as if she were in church.

The sisters' eyes droop and close. The lights are heavy upon them. The noise of the traffic outside, the whirring of electric fans, the whispering in the hall and their certainty about what is being held back carry the sisters deeper into sleep. The tastes of the various dishes are on their tongues. The high arms of their tall chairs make the three sisters appear to be held.

Telly comes back into the house to find the three asleep in their chairs. As Telly passes them to kneel before the casket, Maria Esperanza wakes up.

"Telly? Have you eaten? Where have you been? The Monsignor came to say Mass for your uncle and you were not here," Maria Esperanza chides her.

Telly turns to her aunt. The stiff fabric of the *baro* and *panuelo* stick into Telly's arms with the sharpness of pins.

"He said the Mass in Latin," Maria Paz wakes up, too. "It was beautiful to hear. It was so holy. Did you stay awake during the Mass?" She turns to Maria Caridad, reaching for her arm and shaking it.

"Who?" Maria Caridad asks, waking up.

"The Monsignor. He said Mass this evening."

"Yes," Maria Caridad answers. "When we were children, he used to string ropes on the stairs in order to trip us." The memory fires her smile, for she takes pleasure in recounting the notoriety of the Monsignor's childhood. "I did not believe it when he entered the seminary. Telly, did you know he has confessed all the presidents? He has said Mass in Malacanang except for this one. Perhaps because . . . what is he? Is he prime minister or president or both?"

Maria Esperanza pulls herself up on Telly's arm. "Come. Eat something. You're so thin. I can't see what's holding up your dress. Your mother used to be thin herself. Her wedding dress had to be pinned to her, tied. Come and I will have something with you. I had *pinakbet* made specially for us. You should come and live with me so someone can watch over you . . ."

Maria Paz does not watch them approach the table. She is still thinking of the Mass, thinking of all the Masses she attended when she was a child who walked to church with her mother long before the first rooster crowed. The special darkness attending their devotion seems to pervade the house, and she feels very much consoled.

"Just soup," Telly tells the servant after her aunt has ordered her plate to be heaped with everything on the table.

"Soup! That's just water, Telly. No wonder you're so thin. Try the *relleno* and the *pinakbet*. I smelled the servants stewing the *pinakbet* for themselves and I ordered them to save the pot for us." She has a weakness for eggplants and okra and all the cheap vegetables cooked with fermented shrimp and pork fat. Often, in her house she exchanges the chicken and pork chops for whatever the servants cook for

154

their meal. Sometimes, she goes to the kitchen to pick from their plates.

The sight of the food being placed on her plate makes Telly cringe, yet she accepts it, remembering all the times she had been made to sit at the table, to stare at the lunch she had refused. She looks into her aunt's face, happy in anticipation of food, and notices the rim of blue around the pupils of her aunt's eyes. My own eyes will turn to gray, Telly thinks, looking away at the mirror across the table. Did people notice her eyes fading, too?

"Eat the chicken," Maria Esperanza pushes the *relleno* closer to Telly's fork with her own. "Just take a bite and see how good it is. Don't be stubborn like Severino's son. I don't think he has sat at the table since the wake. Such a strange boy. Don't you think so? There must be something he wants, don't you think? At least something he needs. He can't live on holy water and the Host and the hope of heaven! That I'm sure of. I'm glad none of my children pester me that way. A hospice out of this house! Jaime is going to Europe next week. He's lucky I have something to give him, because he never wins at poker. When I'm gone, who'll see to his needs? Try the *pata*. It's very good."

"I ate before," Telly lies, enjoying the explanation because her aunt has no way of contradicting it. She bites her tongue before she can say that Jaime was at the Mass for imprisoned writers. Her aunt has enough aggravations.

"Well, you can eat again."

Telly turns to her plate. Her aunt speaks as if it is a sin not to eat. In the two days of the wake, Telly is sure the three sisters have devised outrageous sins for her as well. They reconstruct geneologies according to their current whims. In her absence, they would have put their heads together in nonsacramental confession for her. They credit me with sins they dare not commit, having been disappointed that I will not stay locked in my house like a widow; or remarry, if I will not spurn the world. Telly pushes the food together on her plate, making it appear partly consumed.

The wake has been a strange Book of Hours, just as their lives are: full of leisures and secrets but very few mysteries; unending negotiations and reconciliations and breaking apart again; somehow purged of tragedies and real grief. Vital and cardinal decisions are few when survival and salvation mean the same, when in these critical times they cannot see themselves as exiles from heaven, exiles in their own country.

We are all open to failure/Each life is costly to itself/And really, all relationships are fragile.

A Book of Strange Hours/Locked/By Self/Drowned in grace.

Stop, she makes herself take back the words. Poems are just another caprice, a flimsy effort to appear short of breath. I will hear no more from you, she tells herself; and takes the chicken. It is impossible to swallow. The small piece fills her mouth and she cannot breathe.

She is angry at her anger. If you will live/Play by the rules/Eat-drink/Or the world becomes/Paradise enclosed/Exhausted/A fist of hurts.

When she looks up from herself, she sees Paeng coming. She looks past him to the altar, past that to her thoughts as if lying awake in her sleep.

"Tita," he leans across the table. "We have to open the coffin." He sees Maria Esperanza. Not having planned to have her listen to what he has to say, he drops his voice. "I think he was killed. Something I found out at the Mass makes me think so."

Maria Esperanza continues to chew. It takes her time to absorb what she hears. When the words become clear in her mind, she stares at Paeng. It is what she wanted to do from the beginning; but what she will not allow now. "Preposterous. I will not allow my brother to be disturbed just before his funeral."

"But, *Lola*," Paeng pleads. "If he has been ordered killed, should we not know so we can do something?"

"What?" Maria Esperanza asks. "What can we do?"

"We can find out first, if this is true. Should we not let Father Sevi decide?"

"I don't know if he'll return tonight. Besides, it will just disturb things. Everything is arranged, then this fuss. I can't understand you young people. All you want is to disturb us. What good will it do now? You cannot bring him back, can you?"

The hush that falls upon the house when Sevi comes up makes them turn to the stairs. Paeng goes to him. Telly gets up, too, reaches Sevi after Paeng has talked to him. They stand together, their shadows falling together on the floor.

"Telly," Sevi calls.

She looks up, hearing him say her name.

As if they have decided without speaking, their anger and helplessness and fear having joined and become one, they approach Maria Esperanza at the table in the long hall.

When they reach her, suddenly Maria Esperanza cannot put the food into her mouth. She tries to lift the spoon, but it remains on her plate. She stares at it while the light blooms somberly upon it. Wish and fear have become unbearably one for her. And an incantation of broken words comes to her with the realization that something, suddenly, has ended.

# BOOK THREE: Thursday

# 1

Each time they think Maria Esperanza has fallen asleep, she starts walking from one to another of those who are staying up one last night for Don Severino Gil, asking them something they cannot understand. She walks from window to window as on a pilgrimage where the roads are inside her, turning unexpectedly, rising and falling like slopes to be climbed. When she stops, those who are following her in case she falls, stop short. For long periods she stands, in her mourning clothes, as still as a stump without branches, waiting for leaves and flowers to come out of her again.

Telly cries. She sits down, putting both legs under her and covering her knees with her skirt. No one recalls ever seeing her cry. Finina comes over to place both arms about her, sits on the arm of the chair holding Telly. At the last moment, Finina decided to stay for the night. Used to her whims, expecting his own to be allowed, her husband agreed to bring her a change of clothes in the morning. Telly shrinks within her cousin's arms, sits lower in the chair, like a wax candle burning down.

Inside the house, the lights are unfocused, like moonlight. As the night deepens, they brighten off and on as the electricity surges erratically, only to become shallow again as the sun starts coming up over the buildings on Recto.

Sevi is standing beside his father's casket. The windows shelled in *capiz* remain closed and they are all breathing one another's breath, heavy with various scents. Several times over during the night he has changed his mind because he does

161

not know what his father would have wanted. Was it a ruse, that woman's voice telling him his father wished his casket closed? Had he been closer to his father, perhaps he would now know better. What he is certain of is that he should have come to his father; come without being asked, come running; claimed him instead of waiting to be claimed.

His back to the hall, Sevi cries quietly. Was it pride all along that made him want to be a priest, that kept him a priest: weakness hiding in weakness?

The hall is quiet with many silences. The traffic outside has slowed down to an occasional truck. Almost ten years before, students in the thousands had run past that house from the armed forces and Metrocom and police. Don Severino had ordered the large door to the street opened to allow them a hiding place after they had besieged the President at his palace in Malacanang: asking him to be better than himself. Perhaps it was asking too much of an ordinary man.

The quiet in the house matches the hush after the sound of the students' running. Having failed to make Congress listen to their protests, they had marched to the presidential palace where contingents of the armed forces waited, with all the weaponry provided by American military aid, to savage them.

Maria Esperanza comes in from the *azotea* where the drying flowers are heaped together like so many stones. She does not walk so much as she moves, almost as if no bones are holding her up. Followed by her sisters, she approaches Sevi.

He bends over her to catch the words she is saying softly, expecting their wishes to collide in him.

"Severino, tell them," Maria Esperanza hangs on to Sevi's arm. "Tell them I must wear the clothes I wore when I was Maria Elena. The crown and the necklace and the crucifix. The white *saya*. Tell them. I want to get dressed now. It is time to go." Past harboring grief, Maria Esperanza has returned to the high festival of innocence and peace, thinking of all the flowers that she has seen bloom.

Moved that his aunt will come to him like a child awakened

by the night, a child afraid to be put back to sleep, Sevi catches her hands in his. He wonders what she has in mind.

Telly comes forward to join them. He tries to tell her what he thinks their aunt wants. Together they try to know the meaning of words that do not speak themselves, that fail reason and common expectations. Telly feels as if they are riding past large trees on a long road, entering and leaving the shadows.

It is sixty and more years ago, they think, holding Maria Esperanza between them. Her hair is a silver haze above her ears. They hold her up while she looks from one of them to the other. A memory like a relic eludes them: Elena, mother of Constantine, seeker of the true cross.

They bring her to a chair; and there morning catches them. As the first light of the sun comes up against the shells on the windows, Maria Esperanza wakes up, starts pulling off the dark clothes that hold her body. Impatient of promises, she demands to be changed right then and there into her white gown.

It is now that Sevi knows he must allow his father's casket to be opened. Not at the gravesite where it will be opened briefly, barely, then sealed again. He looks up to let Telly know.

And Telly knows also. Now? She asks.

"Now," he answers, knowing that he is sending many mourners away with that decision. But if Paeng is right, they must know immediately. If it is as they suddenly fear, then the casket must be carried open through the streets to La Loma: open so the crime will proclaim itself and its perpetrators.

Fears converge again upon them. "Open through the streets! The police will stop us," Attorney Sandoval predicts. "We will not reach the cemetery before we are all arrested. And for what? Nothing will come of it. And perhaps it is not what you fear. Nothing of that sort really happens any more. And it is only the excess of one person, over zealous in his duty, not the excess of the government. I don't think you'll

163

find what you expect. Go ahead. Open it." The lawyer expects them to yield to the reasons of his pleading; if not to that, then to his dare. "Let us honor the dead."

Those very words make Sevi certain of what he must do. "Let us honor the dead," he repeats, calling the servants to come forward and open the casket. Why not! An act of violence to man desecrates God, blasphemes Him. In his anger he quotes the Proverbs, seeing the verses as clearly as if the Bible were opened on the page. Honor the dead or we kill them twice.

"If I can understand how Paeng can be carried away by what he hears, what he thinks he hears," Attorney Sandoval says, his hand held up while the wreaths are being removed from the casket. "But, you, Father Sevi, I expected..." He has to stand aside to allow more of the wreaths to be removed, laid against the chairs of those who have stood up out of their sleep.

"I'm glad I don't have sons to disturb my final rest," an uncle admonishes Sevi to reconsider. He stands protectively in front of the sisters shielding them. "Must this be done in their presence, too?"

Someone has found a white gown for Maria Esperanza. A servant is kneeling where she stands, putting up the hem.

"Why give in to her?" Attorney Sandoval asks. "She cannot come to the cemetery in that!" he tries to reason with their bewildered hearts. "How can Severino forgive me, if I allow this to take place? Many will refuse to go to the cemetery with her dressed like that."

No one has an answer to that. Telly wants to go over to her aunt, who reminds her of the woman at the hospital in Katonah who kept waking up at night, kept begging for medication which she thought gave her good dreams. Telly herself wants to be out in some garden, in the *azotea*, to be alone; to be wrapped and folded in sleep. The closed casket is her uncle's gift to them; his will, in order not to be dead in their memories as well. This way he will forever be awaited, one still able to come because not seen wrapped in satin. I will not look, she tells herself. God, she begins . . . but does not know how to ask.

"Dona Esperanza, is this what you want?" Attorney Sandoval faces the eldest sister of Don Severino, and the other two sisters through her. They are standing behind her, waiting for things to happen.

"Yes," she says, looking down at the white gown being hemmed up; at the folds that fall about her feet like loose petals. "Yes."

"These must be construction nails," the servant says, failing to pry open the lid of the casket. "I'll look for another hammer. Maybe what I need is a crowbar." His teeth are far apart, and sharp like barbed wire.

"Will that not scar the casket?"

"God's eternal mercy!" Attorney Sandoval says without looking towards the altar. "Everyone has gone mad. Sevi! You must stop this at once. As soon as everyone comes, I suggest we have the Mass and then the funeral; and then just go home in peace afterward. Severino would be outraged. Neither he nor I could stand people to whom everything is either an act of faith or a matter of conscience. They overreact."

Telly stands aside to let Paeng come closer. He has not said a word, as if contrite about causing the agony they are going through.

"And you, young man," Attorney Sandoval notices Paeng, "see what comes of your speaking out! People should have opinions, yes, but they should keep them to themselves." He is so angry that he is speaking now as if his mouth were full of beer, jabbing the air with his fingers. He is accustomed to using a cigar to emphasize a point, but he does not have the time to look for one, to pull its cellophane apart and light it.

Those who disappeared the day before to have their hair done, their nails polished for the funeral, are starting to arrive. They appear sad, not so much from the emotion as from the quality of the light in the hall. The windows have still not been opened.

The new arrivals linger near the stairs, unaware of what is happening near the altar. The men are asking for coffee. They do not think anything can happen to disturb them, because they possess the contentment of those who make money even while they sleep; whose most courageous talk is about motel-hotels in Milan and Copenhagen and the progressive cities of Europe where there are mirrors in the ceilings so one need not miss any part of one's adulteries.

Someone is explaining that he has not come back permanently. "In the States, I've discovered how good it is to work. Here, I wait for the harvest, like government clerks waiting for their salaries. There, I design condos, supermarkets, dentists' chairs." What he says, and the way he says it in earnest, causes much laughter among those who do not believe him. They think him intoxicated.

Aurelio Gil arrives in a fresh suit and a Panama hat. He walks through those at the table, intent on telling the sisters what occurred to him on the way to the wake. "If Sevi will not have his church repaired, and I have no reason to dissuade him, let's use the money for stone angels. There should be enough for all the twelve apostles sculpted out of Romblon marble, to surround his grave . . . " His voice drops when he sees Don Severino's face inside the just opened casket.

Telly is hiding behind both hands, but her heart tears at the sound of her uncle Aurelio's cry, the sound of birds with wings of stone, attempting to fly.

Sevi and Paeng stand silently, seeing bruises as large as staring eyes distort Don Severino's face. The hair is hacked above the ears; part of a lobe is missing. The lips are pressed against impossible pain. How much do his clothes hide?

"That is not Severino," Maria Caridad says, standing up from peering close at her brother. "Where did he get that black suit? He always wore white, with a handkerchief in his breast pocket."

166

"He suffered," Maria Paz says, breathing hard, as if trying to fly out of her mourning clothes. She is trying to recall how he looked alive. How tall was he, and how did he speak? Where did he keep his hands?

Maria Esperanza kicks the servant hemming her white gown to fit her. "Take your hands off me. Go get white flowers to bind the crucifix I will carry. Go. At once."

After a while, with the hall gathered carefully as if within a tight cage, the servant lifts his arms to put the lid in place again.

"Leave it the way it is," Sevi intervenes, without moving toward the casket.

The servant smiles. Then backing away returns to the kitchen where, on the sill, he has left his cigarette to burn another ugly gouge like a slug.

"The way it is? Lord and Savior!" Attorney Sandoval appeals to the sisters to take a hand. "Who will accompany the casket open like that? People along the way will see and ask, who did this? Why? And all sorts of questions. How? In whose name and for what reason? All manner of questions that will raise even more questions. And what reason can we give?"

"It's not for us to give the reason or provide an excuse," Aurelio Gil says. "As to who will accompany Severino to his grave, I will."

"We will not be able to go one block without being stopped. And then what? Curfew again? Detention? Censorship? And more Don Severinos. I will have nothing to do with this. I will not wish the return of terror for others." Attorney Sandoval steps back.

The family remains silent. Telly feels she is driving full tilt up some mountain and the road is sliding away from her. She is afraid for Sevi and Paeng, for the three sisters.

"Father Sevi?" Attorney Sandoval asks for the son to relent.

"It will remain open," Sevi answers.

"Then you cannot blame the government for what happens next." Attorney Sandoval looks around for support. "The government gets blamed for what individuals have done. We don't even know if the President knows of this, much less ordered it. He is too busy with matters of policy and grave concern to all..."

The light falls upon Attorney Sandoval like an oppressive body mask. Many believe his explanations, wait to have the casket resealed. But Aurelio Gil still has something to say.

"Why not? Why not, Attorney? The arrogance of the President in assuming powers he gives to himself makes it possible for tyranny to seep down. He has constitutional powers only because he changed the Constitution to give himself those powers. Anyone with imperial instincts models himself after the one in Malacanang, making and interpreting the laws to his advantage. So many little dictators all over the country, clones of the one in Malacanang. And no recourse against any of them." He presses against them with the whole length of his thoughts and they squirm. "With what will we overcome inequities and oppression?"

"Vote Capuchoy for President/Prime Minister," Paeng is sarcastic. "Or take heart that everything will be all right as long as we hope in heaven. Democracy will fall upon us like manna from the sky. The Pope is coming. Long live the Philippines. The Bible says obey authority. Does it mean unlawful rulers, too?"

"Never. We are asked to save ourselves," Aurelio Gil says, urging Sevi to speak by throwing an arm about him. "Saving ourselves is possible because Christ came into history. If we believe in Him, we will not tolerate absolute rulers on earth. We will resist..."

What must have happened to Don Severino is described in varying exactitudes as new mourners come up for the funeral. Fears and disbelief multiply with each telling. as people press forward to see what will give them nightmares.

Sevi stands among them, his white cassock expanding the

light coming into the hall from the street, holding them precariously where they stand together, as if away from the bars of a cage. To Telly he looks powerful because of his decision to open the casket, to have it remain open. She sees him as the one who joins their lives now, the one awaited who gives them a cause. Even as she thinks this, she knows it can be a bold exaggeration. They are all of them blank Books of Revelation, with human weakness and frail hearts.

The Monsignor arrives to celebrate the last Mass for Severino Gil. They assemble quickly. Standing full of concern they occupy dissimilar spaces.

The Latin sounds strangely votive and dark, incantations meant to seal mysteries even farther from the human heart, but the older relatives revel in it as in a forbidden delicacy. The old priest lifts lined hands, holds them over their heads in blessing, giving them time to consider if they will join the funeral or go home after the final offering of respect to Don Severino in his house.

It is hot in the hall. It is as if they were out in the open field, subject to the sun and wind, with their eyes tearing from the dust. Some leave right away, and the sisters' fear that there might not be enough food after the funeral proves to be unnecessary after all. At the end of the ritual the hall could be a town where half of the people have moved away.

The wreaths take their place. More are being brought up for people coming for the first time. They will only have to be brought down again, but the gesture is important, part of the gracious old ways. Trucks to carry away the flowers are lined along the sidewalk. The flowers drying in the *azotea* have been hauled off to be loaded on a government plane and dropped over the grave during the rites. Maria Esperanza's son, who is a general stationed in Cagayan, has arranged it.

For the last time the servants take a look at the body inside the coffin. Then it is wheeled around and carried toward the stairs. Loud sobbing comes from them, lined along the staircase as the family begins to descend.

It takes time to carry the sisters down the stairs. They are heavy in their grief. Their feet fail to alternate properly on the steps.

In the same dress of the day before, Telly walks behind them. Alongside, cousins in clothes ordered especially for the funeral put the flowers to shame. Who wears black any more?

Outside, passersby stop to look into the casket being loaded onto the open hearse. Occupants of buses stalled in front of the house look out of their windows. The screeches of jeeps and buses distracted by what is seen from the avenue sound like stifled wails. The windshields of passing trucks thrust the sun to the door of Don Severino's house where the family stands, waiting for their cars. The anxiety of those under the portico formed by the upper floor chills the sun. It is as if someone dies every minute they are standing there.

Where the wreaths stood on the sidewalk the members of a band wait to board the bus that has brought them. There is some argument about keeping the band, about whether it should follow the funeral or merely play at the cemetery. The younger ones think the band too provincial. But the sisters have insisted on at least one band. Papá had two, they recall: the one from Pasig and the one from Malabon. The oddness of their request gives it the air of final wishes to which the younger ones defer.

The funeral procession starts slowly. Since their last dead, the traffic pattern has changed. Now they must take into account the high concrete barricades that keep pedestrians from crossing at intersections, that can contain demonstrators and seal escape.

It is a lonely way. Telly has absolutely no words left to respond to the loss and distortions facing them; to give her feelings speech, so she will not feel forbidden, like someone who lies buried under another name. There is only the sound of broken, interrupted silence. I will never think poems again, she tells herself. Is this what her doctor in Katonah saw in her future? Is he thinking of her now?

170

Nor can she cry. In order to focus herself, she keeps track of her three aunts in the car ahead while Sevi sits to her right, his sacred robes on his arm. Paeng is beside the driver.

They are not stopped. Traffic policemen see the motorcycle escorts, also arranged for by Maria Esperanza's son, and stop traffic for them. Remote from everything but their order to accompany the funeral cortege, the escorts do not even notice the people looking down from their windows. Telly watches for a change of expression, a sudden movement to betray thought.

"We used to be able to see La Loma from here," Telly remembers. "At least the fields that sloped down to the cemetery, the rise where the seminary stood like a small hill itself. The mountains of Marikina were close enough then to be able to see the crowns of single trees." Or had that been a dream, distance become deniable, as alterable as modern truth?

Once they pass Blumentritt there are ugly buildings hiding the fields. The old market has been razed, and trade is now lodged in a large building without color. Telly recalls the train crossing where vendors, spilling out into the streets, used to offer their baskets to the passengers at the windows.

"It used to be beautiful going to La Loma," she tells Sevi. "We picked off flowers from the grass. Weed flowers but nevertheless pretty. We used to go with picnic baskets early in the morning of All Saints' Day. At night, the priests began blessing the graves again..." She talks softly about all the things she knows by heart.

He does not have those memories. Sevi looks ahead. The sun is scattered on the waxed roofs of the preceding cars. Psalms occur to him: Happy are they whose strength you are, Father/Who dwell in your house...He wonders if he will continue to live among strangers. What have I done to my father?

Past the gate of the cemetery that is flanked by large stone angels and statues of heroes commissioned for town plazas, displays from the lapidary shops on Avenida Rizal Extensión, the sisters' car stops to allow them to walk some token distance to the graveside. A man at each arm helps them. They appear to float, their black velvet slippers beating down the dust. Coarsely dressed children run alongside the hearse. Curious passersby join them, making up for relatives and friends who chose not to come along.

Paeng holds the car door open for Telly, then he and Sevi walk on beside her. He is wondering how many wounds the dark, ill-fitting suit on Don Severino conceals, whether vengeance is the only possible exertion of his love. Clouds, like branches of large acacias pressed against the sky, float above them.

Telly recalls that beside her mother's grave there used to be a pond. She tells this to Sevi. "I wonder if it overflows when it rains?" She does not expect him to know. Where does water flow? She wishes she had changed her dress, had a veil. What a terrible thought, she swiftly castigates herself. She should be thinking of her uncle, of herself not at all. There was a beautiful girl at the hospital in Katonah who asked for medication every hour on the hour. "The pills are no good for my head," she told Telly, "but they're fantastic for my nails."

Don Severino Gil's face in death is a fire trapped smouldering in Paeng's thought. "Once," he says, "Lolo Severino asked me if I wanted to be a lawyer like my father. It was at a wedding. I was ten and a ringbearer. All I was thinking about was the matchbox filled with coconut beetles that I had seen a boy holding as we filed into church."

Jaime catches up with them. "I'll be saying Mass for Tio Severino this afternoon at the Archbishop's chapel. Will you be there, Telly?"

"I've heard so many Masses the past two days," Telly says. She feels very tired, just wants to be by herself, to think of everything that has happened, of what never will; impatient to live before these past days, to return to when her uncle was alive, though she cannot remember what she was doing Sunday. Or Monday. Is it because her life is fractured by what she does and what she means to do; because there is no fixed point, no one person...? "Do you promise a perfect Mass, Jimmy?"

"Every Mass is perfect, Telly." Jaime glances at Sevi. "No matter if the priest wanders into the wrong Eucharistic prayer, or becomes distracted; Jesus is concelebrating. No way can it be flawed. Telly, we don't have to act pierced for..."

"So I get scolded for lapses in my Christian training. I'm too old to learn, Jaime." What she wants to say is that she will be there, for her uncle's sake.

"I'm awkward with words, Telly. With feelings. I meant that we all burn with a great fire at the altar, but we're also human, with none of the perfection people demand in order to be led into belief. He chose the weakest, the least to be His disciples." Jaime lets Telly walk ahead, to wait for his mother, who is struggling alongside her sisters, impeded in her walking by the long gown that is coming apart at the hem. As she comes up, he places an arm about her while thinking of Telly, devising an opportunity to tell her, "Be gentle. Be gentle with yourself."

Finina has stopped to wait for Telly; and her own brood of daughters and sons, annoyed, wait impatiently for her to return. "Remember now, Telly. Geneva in April. With Susan. It will bring color to our cheeks."

As if Tio Severino is not being buried! Telly says to herself. As if we're on a long walk to the river where we'll wet our feet and then climb up the star-apple trees. Is it from fear or grief that they are distracting themselves? What can be learned from suffering that can be discovered without going through it? It feels as if birds in finely woven cages are hanging about them. Don Severino has made something possible, which she does not understand. He never seemed so alive as then, with them in what feels like perfect memory, in which she can linger at will, safe from the anger and helplessness and also joy, indistinct in her heart.

They arrive at the graveside with the sun almost centered

173

in the sky. Each sister's hair has blown stiff in the wind, free of the clutch of combs, standing out as if each shock they have ever endured has left its claws in them.

There is a commotion when the hearse stops in front of the dug earth banked beside the road, away from the chairs upon which no one will sit. Finally, the escorts see the open casket. They dismount from their motorcycles to order it closed, but do not insist when the Monsignor and the priests of the family stand around it, making a protecting cave of their bodies. Foreign correspondents, plotting their coverage of the Pope's routes, have stumbled upon the funeral and begin popping flashbulbs. Attorney Sandoval steps away to the edge of the mourners.

Outside the tent raised over the grave, there is no shade in which to stand. The sun is hot and direct. It is new ground being broken, out in the open where there are few trees on which a bird may alight. The family had decided to reinter all their kin under one roof. Designed to be circular so everyone would be equally placed, the roof will not be constructed until later, to be finished by the next first of November, All Saints' Day.

A plane circles overhead, flies away, then starts coming with its load of flowers.

Telly feels herself ebbing away, her heels sinking into the porous ground, the grass thin and without roots. She stares at the casket, forcing herself to look into it. Her wish to die — is it the one constant in her life? — returns. Soon enough/It will happen/Why cry like birds/With beaks clinging to summer? She is reminded of waterfalls. Those on the way up to Baguio are not seen to reach the earth. She recalls aunts throwing themselves into the graves of husbands and children, attempting to, and only falling into the arms of relatives who braced themselves for such outbursts. She has no grave upon which to throw herself.

Crosses set up the previous All Saints' are already overgrown with weeds. She recalls one such day among many, pulling wildflowers by the handful and looking up to see a sepulcher's dark emptiness open.

Two graves down and upon unsuspecting shrubs, the flowers drop from the plane. Amused by the error, some smile, fully expecting that it will be repeated.

The plane prepares to make another sweep while the Monsignor begins the rites.

He is saying, "We entrust Severino to God whose chosen people we all are; to God who will never abandon us. Nothing can separate us from His love: neither death nor life, neither angels nor other heavenly powers; neither the present nor the future; neither the world above nor the world below. There is nothing in all creation that will ever be able to separate us from the love of God which is ours..."

The plane is coming over them again. Photographers get ready to take pictures of petals falling upon the grave.

"Can trouble separate us, or hardship, or persecution, or hunger, or poverty, or danger or death? For creation was not doomed to be worthless. There is this hope, that creation will one day be set free from its slavery...We have nothing to fear. God is among us, God, our only overlord..."

The children are being lifted across the open casket that is set to be lowered into the grave. The ritual symbolizes the hope that they will be able to cross safely the chasms that will tear apart their lives. The smallest makes no sounds. But Telly catches the look on the face of a little girl who is secretly wiping the holy water that has sprinkled her face, so wonderfully pure, it seems to Telly; as if reflected on a pearl.

To keep from crying Telly glances up at the sky that overflows with light. She attempts to bring her thoughts down to what is happening, but her mind struggles. Sacrificed birds/ The odor of uprooted hills/Light that falls short of the fields. Her doctor said it is the struggle that saves us. But how does a life become a living sacrifice? No poem will come again to her, she fears. The words disappear as they come. Too many wounds slay her.

The trees, what there are of them in the distance, are like nets spread to catch the universe should it fall. The sun is a white hole in the sky.

Telly looks for Sevi, sees him looking at her the way he looked up from the chalice at the first Mass he celebrated in his father's house. She cannot bear it and looks away, back to what the Monsignor is saying. The Monsignor's words hurt, as if they originated inside her instead of in scripture. She has never loved God back, nor properly another. How is it her feelings for her Uncle Severino have led her to Sevi; and from Sevi . . . will it lead to God? She is trembling, shaking as if her arms are being lifted for her.

Or am I exaggerating even more than ever? She has never felt this full of grace, of peace despite their common anguish, despite her knowledge that their lives will never allow . . . will always be apart; but the straining towards/away from the other will be their bond. And because she loves him, she need not love anyone else, or even be loved back.

A third time the plane is flying low with the last flowers from the wake. Petals hang in the air, like ricebirds. Awaiting their hovering fall, Telly sees Quiel, or someone who looks like him, a face shadowed by itself, standing with the mourners on the other side. Because her fine yearning is not for him, she does not recall pain or anger.

Alone, not alone, she feels complete, not needing the fluctuating happiness of dreams. The walls of earth opening gently to the sky do not remind her of death. The hatred is finally gone, she tells herself; gone from the moment at least; and there is only affection, or peace, and maybe forgiveness but she is not sure. If it is possible to love God through man, might it not be possible to love man through God?

Strangely, these thoughts comfort her. When she closes her eyes, a sound of flowers falling, or of sap rising, comes to her. Out of the petals drips light as sweet as bees. Oddly she feels she is in several places, traveling toward even more silence while the whisperings about her become mouths capable

176

of astonishment with the playfulness of angels. She recalls Saint Agnes' antiphon/responsory: When I shall have loved Him, I shall be chaste; when I shall have touched Him, I shall be clean . . .

The words come to her with the strength of surging waves as she stands braced against the casket. She thinks she will write after all about the family, gather them together; write about the nephew braver than she, who told her of young girls he has seen tied to stakes in Samar by government agents, then sliced vein by vein with razorblades, even their eyes at last. It will not have his fury, for lack of her having witnessed it; but she will write until he can – when agents no longer follow him or search his house; or in case he even gives up writing. She will write it as a tale of what happens when men mutilate justice in their own country. Will this story include forgiveness? It will be about her uncle, too; it will be *for* him. In remembrance. She will let the words in her mind out into the world.

If life is really a pilgrimage, its purpose cannot be only safety or comfort. And the Pope himself is a pilgrim taking the risk that someone might try to kill him in Manila the way that Peruvian painter slashed at Pope Paul. And God possibly is a pilgrim wandering among us, inside each of us looking for a place of rest, in which to be reborn. Then the sign of His presence cannot be wealth and abundance but the willingness to accept suffering . . .

Off to one side the band is playing softly. The children are pulling at the hands that are holding them in place beside the three sisters of Don Severino. Aurelio Gil has brought fresh *sampaguita* necklaces to place on the casket after it is closed.

But how shall I write about Tio Severino? Telly wonders. Already she is frightened by the effort she will have to make. In the end/How can Saint Peter/Find out which war killed which/By the wounds perhaps?/Or who/Succumbed to which government/Foreign or their own?

It's strange, Telly thinks, looking up to where the plane has flown above and disappeared. I did not see any birds. And what will Sevi say? Like his father, will he inform me that submission makes a woman beautiful and desired?

She is besieged by the urgency to understand everything and at once; to be beyond mere being. So far, she hopes, she has escaped being just an elegant fact, a glimmering numeral, an imagination without an imagining self. She wants to find what life cannot exhaust, and to which it returns from death; to know all the things she has resisted knowing.

The three sisters of Don Severino finish their laments. They turn to one another, all that is left, their hands grasping each other's arms. They become tangled in their crying.

For the last time, cousins come to them and grandchildren kiss their hands. Not everyone chooses to return to the houses of the bereaved for the final meal.

In another minute they are led toward their car, which has followed them to the graveside, thereafter to be taken for the last time to Don Severino's house for the reception. Until the next wake, they will not sit at the family table again. And if it is turned into a hospice, where will their next wake be held?

Telly turns to leave with them. Before joining her aunts she is tempted to look down into the casket that is now covered with earth, but she cannot do even that. Yet she is glad that Sevi decided to open the casket; that she did not ask him to bury the truth.

Because she did not look into his open casket, she will be able to remember her uncle with a fine gardenia in his lapel, face scented with baby powder, a large diamond tie pin that, when asked to explain, he says is to ransom him should the need arise.

She has a choice. She can remember him that way, or among the rosebushes in the garden of his house on Recto. Once there was every kind of tree and shrub there...

With breathtaking clarity she is seeing him through what others have remembered of him during the wake. Is this what life is about, to strengthen one another when one's own strength fails? Or she can recall the cry of those who looked bravely into his casket and saw his face . . .

Paeng hurries after her. His face is solemn with the certainty that until it happens, they will have to continue to fear what might happen to them because they opened Don Severino Gil's casket and carried it exposed through the public streets. He knows he has forced many to make a stand, as if he had the right to demand a sacrifice from others.

Someone will have to pay for what they have done. He is willing to answer for all of them, to pay at that very moment, at the gate, on the way back to the house: whenever and wherever the exaction is made. Even priests have been shot, by hired killers, for standing up to unjust authority; and Bishop Claver has asked, ''What can we do without being God's avenging angel? The line between justice and revenge can become very thin.'' But if his uncle's death is forgotten, someone else will have to die again.

On passing Telly, Paeng holds out his hand to her. She hesitates, then takes it, gives her other hand to Susan who is walking by, even as Paeng reaches out for Maria Caridad's hand and she for her sister Maria Paz who is already holding on to Maria Esperanza.

Their grief, Telly thinks, has become very much like the singing cries of birds; and she hangs on tightly to the hands holding hers. The heads of all I love/Are bones/Down my back/Life-locked/We bleed life's breaths/Sometimes my body remembers them singing.

She looks up to fix in her mind what she has seen happen. The sky is no longer dark to her; it looks like an empty tree that is beginning to fill with new life, brightening with leaves and promises in an unenclosed garden.

Looking for Sevi a last time, Telly sees him still praying by himself at the grave. The flowers that came too late to be dropped from the plane have been piled up on the raw mound of earth. Jaime, her brother Matias, and the priest sons of Maria Caridad and Maria Paz are walking alongside the Monsignor.

179

Their white cassocks sweep forward with the relentless force of driven rain.